THE PANTHER OF BARACOA

Praise for Bayard & Holmes

"A fantastic spy thriller. Wild adventure, delicious storytelling, tradecraft that only the insiders know. *Apex Predator: The Leopard of Cairo* is an excellent reminder that great spies tell great stories. Do not miss the Truth and Fiction section at the back."

-- Annie Jacobsen, Bestselling Author of *Surprise, Kill, Vanish*; TV Writer/ Producer of Tom Clancy's *Jack Ryan*

———

"Bayard and Holmes's *Apex Predator: The Leopard of Cairo* is everything I love in a story: action, intrigue, exotic locations. Here is a lightning-fast tale of intrigue, lies, and the mother-of-all terrorist plots. Big story, big adventure, big thumbs-up!"

—James Rollins, *New York Times* Bestselling Author of the Sigma Force series

———

"A chilling and realistic glimpse behind the secretive, covert veil. Proof that most have no clue how much others sacrifice and willingly forfeit for the rest of us. A fantastic read!"

—Vicki Hinze, *USA Today* Bestselling Author

Also by Bayard & Holmes

APEX PREDATOR SERIES

The Leopard of Cairo

APEX PREDATOR COMING SOON

The Caiman of Iquitos

The Cobra of Nainital

NONFICTION BY BAYARD & HOLMES

Spycraft: Essentials

Key Figures in Espionage

Key Moments in Espionage

Timeline Iran: Stone Age to Nuclear Age

NONFICTION COMING SOON

Key People & Wars

———

BY PIPER BAYARD

Firelands

———

THE PANTHER OF BARACOA

An Apex Predator Novella

BAYARD & HOLMES

Copyright

Shoe Phone Press
2770 Arapahoe Road #132-229
Lafayette, CO 80026

Copyright © 2022 by Bayard & Holmes

All rights reserved as permitted under the U.S. Copyright Act of 1976. No portion of this publication may be reproduced in any form or by any means—electronic, mechanical, photocopy, recording, scanning, or other—except for brief quotations in critical reviews or articles, without the prior written permission of the author.

Layout design by Piper Bayard.
Cover art created by Piper Bayard and Vicki Hinze. All rights reserved.

This novel is a work of fiction. Names, characters, places, and incidents are either products of the author's imagination or used fictitiously. All characters are fictional, and any similarity to events, organizations, or people living or dead is purely coincidental.

ISBN 978-1-7345597-6-7 (Ebook)
ISBN 979-8-9850482-2-3 (Print)

Printed in the United States of America

First Edition: 2022

22 23 24 25 LSC 5 4 3 2 1

For the unsung heroes . . .
We salute you.

Before the CIA and the OSS, there was a network . . .
Some say it's out there still.

Chapter One

MARTIN WENTWORTH BLACKBURN STEPPED FROM THE passenger side of the '55 Thunderbird convertible, his stomach lurching like he'd just ridden out a hurricane on a Royal Navy frigate. The potholed, winding trails through the Cuban hills seemed more like they were built by an amusement park team than civil engineers. He gripped his side and willed his breakfast to stay in place.

At least it isn't Pakistan.

His stomach relaxed a bit. He rounded the front of the car and opened the door for the elderly man in the driver's seat. Then he leaned down and offered his arm.

Señor Delgado's gray mustache twitched into a grin. "You look a little green, Señor Collins." He took Martin's arm and stood.

Martin retrieved Delgado's cane from the back seat for him. "Do I? I'm sure it's nothing a dram of rum can't cure."

Delgado nodded. "I know the perfect place. Private reserve rum and the best *arroz con pollo* in town."

"Brilliant. Do lead on."

Delgado had made Martin's past two weeks ostensibly

touring cocoa plantations as British Trade Specialist Martin Collins with the Department for Business Innovation and Skills a joy. He could now report back to MI6 that eastern Cuba would, indeed, serve for the insertion and extraction of operatives—critical with Russia pushing to build a military and nuclear base on the island.

His friend John Viera had told him he would love the island and the *Cubanos*. In spite of decades of deprivation under *"el maricón Fidel,"* as Delgado called Fidel Castro, they had not lost their humanity. They were alive, and life mattered to them. They were a balm to Martin's aching soul, and he embraced them with his spirit, even as his UK peerage upbringing caused him to cringe at their overenthusiastic hugging.

He slowed his pace to match Delgado's while they meandered up the street called Malecón, winding along the shore of the Bahía de Miel, the *Bay of Honey*. The noon sun tipped the waves with golden light. The soft swish of the ebbing tide kissed the rocks at the foot of the seawall that edged the road. A warm autumn breeze surged up from the Baracoa coast, ruffling Martin's short blond hair and soothing his senses, ragged after hours of blaring horns at every one of the switchbacks through the hills.

He drew in a deep breath, savoring the jasmine-like scent of mariposa blossoms. No. In spite of the roads born in the bowels of Hades, Baracoa definitely was not the hell pit of Quetta.

They crossed the avenue, dodging the bitaxis—carts propelled by bicyclists—as well as automobiles that could have been plucked from the 1950s. They skirted a horse-drawn cart, benches bulging with European tourists, that was paused in front of the Hotel La Rusa, famous for once housing Che Guevara. The horse raised its tail to do its

The Panther of Baracoa

business, and Martin suppressed a laugh, wishing he had an apple to feed the politically astute animal.

Señor Delgado gestured toward the three-story structure. "Do you need to go inside?" Delgado had honored Martin by lodging him in room 302 of the historical building—*el Che*'s room.

"No, thank you."

They rounded a corner and headed into the town. The hotels and apartment buildings that lined the shore gave way to more modest shops and villas sporting tropical yellows, pinks, and blues with revolutionary graffiti on every third surface. Behind them, the lush jungle hills rose above the old Spanish settlement.

A boy played on the narrow sidewalk under a mural of *el Che* while an old woman near him swept dark sand from the stoop of a bright-orange house. She caught Martin's eye and gave him the welcoming smile he had found common among the islanders from Havana to Santiago. Was she Cuban DGI or Russian FSB?

No. Their agents would not have met his eye.

He acknowledged her smile with a nod, and she continued her work, periodically glancing back his way.

Though it was only midday, the regular Saturday night party on Calle Antonio Maceo was already warming up. Passionate Spanish guitars and Afro-Cuban rhythms flowed around Martin, and an image of Lewis, his successor as station chief in Quetta, came to mind. Martin smiled to himself at the thought of how uncomfortable that prig would be in Cuba. He met all forms of levity with suspicion and disapproval and would certainly purse his lips over people reveling in the streets. *To hell with that ponce.*

Martin's smile disappeared. Was Lewis keeping an eye on the drug lords and slave traders? And what about the

3

Taliban? Martin's chest grew tight. He had gone back and destroyed the cell that had ambushed him and killed three of his men, but he hadn't found the mole that had set them up. Perhaps John had found something on his end?

If only I'd gotten the maggot we caught to talk before he died. If only . . .

No. He couldn't think like that. What was it he always told John? Don't stall. Don't commiserate. The battle is still in front of you. And thank God today's battle was in the paradise of Cuba, securing a deal with Delgado. Russian power and ambition were growing, and Putavich's eyes were on the West. The United Kingdom needed to keep its own eyes on Russia, and for that, MI6 needed a cover operation in Cuba.

Delgado stopped in front of an open café at the edge of the street party. "The best *pollo* in Cuba."

"Excellent." Martin's stomach, now fully recovered from the carnival ride of a drive, rumbled with anticipation of the spicy chicken.

The waiter seated them on a porch surrounded by a low blue-plastered barrier and filled their glasses with the private reserve. Nearby, a growing crowd laughed at the florid jokes the *presentador* at the microphone made when he introduced singers and songs.

Martin studied the European tourists meandering past a few meters away while his companion ordered. *Where is she?* Like a persistent solicitor, a Spanish woman appeared at the edge of a group gathered around some conga drums. He would have been disappointed if it had taken her longer to find him, as she had done every day he spent in town since his arrival. Martin indulged himself in a brief stare, appreciating the contrast her long, black ponytail made against her white bikini and red pareo. Whether she was

The Panther of Baracoa

DGI or FSB, it was a shame either way. Her body was most inviting, but he didn't want to sleep with someone he might have to kill.

Focusing his mind back on the business at hand, Martin fished out a compact humidor from his jacket pocket and offered a short Cohiba cigar to Señor Delgado. Then he selected one for himself.

"*Gracias.* So now you have seen how we love our cocoa. In fact, our production has increased thirteen hundred percent since *Habana* gave us permission to directly export for foreign currency." His eyes twinkled, as they always did when he spoke of chocolate.

Martin laughed. "Really? Thirteen hundred percent? That's rather extraordinary, don't you think?"

Delgado grinned. "Well, perhaps eight percent. The other twelve hundred and ninety-two may have slipped through the Dominican Republic to American mobsters. They take it to Puerto Rico and sell it in the US under counterfeit labels."

Martin raised his eyebrows. Bootleg booze was big smuggling trade in the Caribbean, but bootleg chocolate?

Delgado nodded, obviously pleased to be supplying the "British trade representative" with such important information. "No taxes on the smuggled cocoa. No sugar taxes in Puerto Rico. They use Central American illegals to work in their chocolate factories, which they hide in dairy operations. Much better and cheaper chocolate than *esos tontos en Mejico* make."

Martin flinched internally at the bigotry that was common among various Latin American groups, but in that moment, he was not about to take up the issue of cultural equality.

Señor Delgado lowered his voice and glanced over his

shoulder. "As long as we *say* we hate capitalists, we are allowed to *be* capitalists. *Habana* only wants its cut, and with the American mobsters, it gets nothing." He leaned back in his chair. "*¿Sí?*"

Martin nodded. "*¡Sí!* . . . I notice that Cubans are a bit short on electronics. I'm authorized to offer you first-class British consumer electronics from Brown Microsystems in exchange for your cocoa."

Delgado wrinkled his brow. "I must tell you that the British are not the only bidders. The Dutch sent a representative last week."

Martin puffed his cigar, working to hold his poker face. If the deal fell through, he would be sent to a desk in England, or perhaps even back to Pakistan. The thought felt like receiving a summons from the abyss. He wasn't sure which would be more oppressive. A desk in England would crush his soul in six months, and Pakistan? It would end him in a week. He'd given four years of himself to that cesspool of terror, posing as a Canadian geologist while running clandestine operations, only to be betrayed in the end. The thought of one more minute . . .

Surprised by the strength of his reaction, he shut down his anguish to keep his head clear. He studied the people strolling through the street. The Spanish woman had joined some dancers beside the drums. Her swaying hips promised sultry pleasures with movements as smooth as those of a feral cat. Was she working for the Dutch?

Martin returned his regard to Delgado. "And what did they offer you?"

The Cuban shifted closer. "Flood control is a big problem here. The Dutch know much about such things."

So the Dutch had offered flood-control equipment.

The Panther of Baracoa

How could he use that? "Flood-control technology is worthless without computers to command the system."

Delgado shook his head. "But computers will not keep the waters at bay."

Damn. What else? "You could sell the computers to purchase the equipment and have a bit left over for yourself."

Delgado sighed. "Señor Martin, I would like to do business with you, but that plan would not leave enough profit for all of the trouble. Why would I want to do that?"

A logical question. Cold, hard cash was sure to change the chap's mind, but MI6 was adamant that Martin had to make the electronics be enough. Brown Microsystems was a huge contributor to the Labour Party, as well as partners with Government Communications Headquarters in electronic surveillance of British citizens and foreigners. Forcing their excess on the Cubans would thank Brown for the information and financing they provided in a way that would shield the intelligence branches and the government from public scrutiny.

The waiter slipped their plates in front of them, and the aroma of chicken seasoned with bay leaf cut through the smoke. Martin tamped out his cigar and took a bite, turning the problem over in his mind. He was not without means. He could invest in the cocoa himself. He was sure to make a profit, and his mother's bankers could handle the exchange discreetly.

A weight lifted from his shoulders, and his heart was light for the first time he could remember. To hell with the jihadis and scumbags in Pakistan, along with the rest of the people who would rather kill than live. He'd done his time in the abyss, and no one could say he hadn't. It was time to retire from the wars and embrace life again. He had always joked with John that he would one day retire in Cuba and devote himself to savoring cigars. That day had come. He would get used to the hugging eventually.

Martin barely stopped himself from laughing with delight at the thought. "How about this? Cash for your cocoa. Whatever the mob pays plus 10 percent to cover the cut for *Habana*, and the surplus computers besides. Then you could purchase the flood-control system and have more than enough profit to justify the trouble. You know the Dutch will never match that. *¿Sí?*"

The elderly Cuban paused, his face blank. Then he grinned. "*¡Sí!* I think that can work. I'll notify the Dutch immediately." He held up his rum. "To British chocolate. *Habana* will be pleased."

"Cheers." Martin clinked his glass, downed his rum, and removed a pen from his breast pocket. He reached for a clean table napkin to write out a draft of the contract. "I'm on a plane for England in two days, but I'll be back by the end of the month. Can your solicitor finish this in time?"

Señor Delgado nodded. "He will prepare it this afternoon. We can meet this evening and sign over dinner."

The *presentador* at the microphone told a joke about Puerto Rican musicians, and laughter erupted in the street. Martin wrote out the agreement, the joyful tones around him echoing the deep contentment spreading through his being. Lawrence was "of Arabia," and it had sucked his brain and soul dry. Pakistan tried to do the same to Martin, but he would not let it. He would be "of Cuba" and live with his mind and soul intact.

Chapter Two

MARTIN PARTED WITH DELGADO AND STROLLED SOUTH down Malecón toward the warm sands of the Playa de Miel, sizing up the shore for night landings with small boats. Then he stopped himself. *That's not my job anymore.*

Standing at the water's edge, he let the solitude lull him, remembering what it was like to simply stand still for a moment. His body relaxed, and he studied the fishing boats bobbing at sea. One had a pod of dolphins playing at its bow. He sighed.

He felt her approach before he saw her. She glided across the sand with the mesmerizing grace of a panther, her black hair flowing loose to her waist. Why did she glance over her shoulder? Did she think someone was watching her?

He shrugged. Not his problem. The only reason anyone would be after him now was to get in on a cut of the cocoa action.

She stopped beside Martin and gazed at the ocean, her red pareo fluttering on the sea breeze, teasing him with a hint of her tan legs. He would have enjoyed the glimpse, but her face was taut and her eyes strained. Martin's senses sprang to life. He shot a look toward the jungle behind them. Was that a face peeking out through the trees?

"DGI?" He kept his voice calm and low.

"*Sí*. But these days, I'm not so sure." Her tones were urgent, but her voice was sweet and clear.

"If all DGI agents are as beautiful as you, I might defect."

She laughed, the sound as nervous as her eyes. "I assure you, señor, most of us are as ugly as your MI6."

Martin chuckled. "How did you know to dress for the beach today?"

Her lips curved up in a small smile, still watching the passing ships. "People always return to this beach. You have been in the hills for most of two weeks. Unless there was a hurricane, you were going to come to the beach today."

She finally faced him, her black eyes intent. "You are MI6 agent Martin Wentworth Blackburn. You were born on an estate in the Kent countryside and educated at Oxford. You began your career in the Balkans and spent your last four years in Pakistan working closely with an American against the Taliban, al-Qaeda, and ISIS, and to rescue your abandoned citizens. This is your first time in Cuba, and you are using your personal finances to secure a deal for your country with Señor Delgado and the cocoa farmers. I know this because your MI6 is far too cheap to pay cash."

His peace evaporated. What did she want? He turned his gaze back toward the sea, where clouds had appeared along the horizon.

She also looked back to the ocean. "*Habana* knows you come to watch the Russians build their big base. It doesn't care. *Ingles, Ruso*—only business deals to *Habana*. Pay a fair

The Panther of Baracoa

price for the cocoa, finance a dock expansion, and England will have chocolate for a hundred years."

She slid a furtive glance over her shoulder again, then whispered, "I am Edurne Montalvo, and I need a favor. You *Ingles* and the *Yanquis* need a favor from me and my friends, too, but you don't know it yet."

Martin swallowed, reluctant to ask the questions he knew he must ask. "What favor do you need? What favor do I need?"

She shifted her posture to spy up the beach, and his skin prickled. Was someone there, or was he simply resonating with her paranoia?

She took his hand and spoke fast. "Take this flash drive. Do not email it from here, or it will be intercepted. Do not trust it to your ministry. Deciphering keys were sent to José-Luis Gonzales, a waiter at Caribe Azul in your Chelsea District. They are disguised as British marketing company pyramid scam tapes. No one will want to watch them. Ask José-Luis, 'Did you go to the baseball game last night?' He will answer, 'No, I went to the basketball game.' Get copies of this information to European and Canadian journalists, and maybe some *Yanquis*. You will know who to trust when you've seen what's here. Without the deciphering keys, this drive will only appear to contain pictures of this beach. Enjoy the pictures, but leave immediately, and never come back to Cuba."

Leave and never come back? Nonsense!

Martin eyed her, his suspicion aroused. "How do I know you aren't working for the Dutch, trying to scare me off this deal?"

"Would the Dutch know what I know about you?"

Martin's heart sank. They wouldn't.

A sudden gust blew her hair across her face, and she

smoothed it back. "It's not safe for you here. Once you pass the information, you will not be safe in the UK, Mexico, Russia, or the US, either. You might even be in danger in the EU."

Martin raised an eyebrow. "Doesn't leave much, does it? You said yourself that I have *Habana*'s blessing, and I like it here. Perhaps I don't want this problem of yours. Did you think of that?"

"I like it here, too, but what we like is not important. What we want is not important, and this is not only my problem. You will understand when you see what I have given you. Too many people will suffer if we do not expose those plans, and you have not spent your life making the world a better place to let this happen."

"What plans? The Russians?"

The Dutch accents of a man and a woman floated across the beach, and Martin spotted a young European couple strolling their direction. The woman pointed toward a large ship on the horizon.

Edurne's eyes widened. "We have stayed here too long together. We were both trained better than this. *Vaya con Diós*, Mr. Blackburn. I must go make a home in a new country."

Martin watched her back while she hurried toward the town, graceful even in her haste. The Dutch couple stared when she passed. Were they spies, too? Or were they only caught by her exotic beauty?

Martin ran his thumb across the USB drive in his palm. He could throw the bloody thing out into the surf and forget about it. The idea was appealing. But Edurne's fear and earnestness had been real, and there was no telling what trouble the world was brewing this time. He already had a ticket booked for England—a quick turnaround just long

The Panther of Baracoa

enough to report to MI6 and to satisfy his mother with a visit. He could at least take it with him and see what was on it.

Martin sighed and ambled up the beach toward the street party in town. When he entered the Calle Antonio Maceo, he automatically surveyed the crowd. For the first time since his arrival in Baracoa, the Cuban-Spanish beauty was nowhere to be found.

Tension pinched his shoulders, and he glanced right and left. The woman he'd seen earlier sweeping the streets was laughing with some friends, her hand holding the little boy who had been playing near her. She looked up at him and smiled. Was she an agent, after all?

He peered back toward the beach. No one. Martin thought of Edurne's warning. It would be another three days before he could connect with José-Luis to get the codes, and if she was telling the truth, it would be best if he sent a cutout rather than go himself. Martin looked down at his left hand and focused on his pinky ring—a silver band with the inscription *Apex Invictus*, "Apex Undefeated." It had been in his family for generations and been on his finger at every opportunity since he turned fifteen.

He sighed. He hated to make that call, but he needed someone he could trust outside of the ministry, and it was best to get the ball rolling.

Martin ducked into a busy restaurant to shield himself from any prying eyes on the street and made a beeline for the men's room, slowing to take advantage of the noisy crowd. He dug out his mobile phone and dialed the one civilian in his personal life who shared his state-of-the-art communications encryption. It rang only once before the eager voice of an older woman came on the line.

"Martin, my boy. Where are you?"

"I can't say at the moment, Mother, but I have a surprise for you."

"You're coming home, getting married, and giving me grandchildren?" She always sounded so hopeful when she said it.

"You know me better than that, but I will be there for dinner this Thursday." He dodged a waiter with a large tray.

"Martin, that's brilliant! I'll let Cook know to expect you. I can't wait to see you. Will you stay at least a few weeks this time?"

"Sorry, Mum, but I won't be more than a few days. I have a pressing business deal that I think will interest you. I can't get into it now, but I need a favor. Could you please send Percival over to Caribe Azul in the Chelsea District to find a waiter there named José-Luis Gonzales?" Martin repeated the code phrases Edurne had given him. "The waiter will give Percival a parcel for me."

She paused, and when she spoke again, her voice was heavy with disappointment. "Very well, he can do that first thing in the morning. Meanwhile, that Domino of yours broke another board out of his stall. I can't believe you sent him all the way from Pakistan. It's not like we don't have a polo pony or two in England. You really should spend more time here to work with him."

Martin's jaw tightened. "Sweet talk him the way you do your investors. I'm sure he'll come around."

"Perhaps I'll have Cook put him in a stew. Shall we have him for dinner Thursday?"

"I have a better idea. Have her pick up a fresh goose, and I'll make my special recipe for you." *At least if I'm in the kitchen, you won't be nagging me.*

The Panther of Baracoa

"The one with the cranberry glaze? You must give Cook your recipe."

"Certainly not. Then what would you need me for?"

"Don't be silly, dear. You know I live and breathe for you . . . I'll schedule a hunt and a game for Saturday. The hounds are keen for an outing and so am I. I'll invite Caroline. I'm sure she would love to see you."

Ugh. Caroline had a longer pedigree than his horse's and wasn't half as smart. Not like . . . No. I have to forget her. "That will be lovely, Mother."

"Be safe. It will be so good to see you."

"And you, as well." It *would* be good to see her. For three days. "Cheers." Martin replaced his phone in his pocket when he reached the men's room. He went inside, washed his hands, and then stepped onto the street. Studying the layout, he renewed his awareness of the shops and avenues, checking again for familiar faces.

Were those two men there a moment ago? They turned away and went into a shop.

He spotted a shack he'd seen earlier sporting ads for hiking tours of El Yunque, the limestone outcropping that Christopher Columbus had described as "a high and square mountain that looks like an island." He crossed to it and said in a loud voice, "When does tomorrow's tour depart?"

The tour guide gave Martin a broad smile. "At sunrise, señor. Shall I add your name?"

"Please do. Martin Collins."

Martin lingered another twenty minutes, chatting with the tour guide about the flora and fauna of the Guantánamo region, making it clear to anyone listening that he planned to stay on the island for a least one more day. If there was anything to Edurne's claims, he didn't want any spies feeling like they had to rush to pick him up.

15

Martin started down the street toward Hotel La Rusa and then doubled back. Listening to the music, he watched the revelers, soaking in the atmosphere of life being lived and loved, and determination rose inside him. No matter what was on the USB, this would not be the end of Cuba for him. He would get back to England and sort this out, and then nothing would keep him away.

Chapter Three

MARTIN SET DOWN HIS PEN BESIDE THE COMPLETED contract and raised a glass with Señor Delgado. "To cocoa, to profits, and to beautiful women to share them with."

Delgado gave a hearty laugh and drank. Their waiter whisked away their dinner dishes to the sound of bongos, congas, batás, and timbales heating up in the *calle*. The crowd cheered. Martin smiled and savored his cigar, eyeing the people passing by in the street below the rooftop-terrace restaurant.

The two men he'd spotted earlier had returned and were laughing with a third friend outside of a nightclub. None of them glanced his way. No sign of the woman and child he'd seen earlier, and no glimpse of Edurne.

His mind went to the USB drive deep in the front pocket of his trousers. *She could be daft.* He consciously chose to relax and anticipate another day in paradise.

"I would like to thank the rest of the Cooperative," Martin said. "I'll hire out La Punta for tomorrow night, and we'll have a fiesta of our own. Bring your wives and families if you like. Do you know a good band?"

"*Sí*. My cousin's son is the best guitar player in all of Guantánamo."

"Brilliant." Martin noticed the men and their friend had disappeared. An old woman stood in their stead, her hunched back and missing teeth doing nothing to dampen her enthusiasm as she clapped with the music.

They stood and Martin handed Señor Delgado his cane. Then Martin raised his voice ever so slightly for the benefit of anyone wanting to hear him. "I'll be hiking El Yunque in the morning, but I'll look forward to meeting with the Cooperative tomorrow night. Seven o'clock?"

"Seven o'clock." Delgado nodded.

Martin held out his hand. Señor Delgado ignored it and took him up in an enthusiastic hug. Martin almost didn't cringe. Then he took Delgado's arm and steadied the old man as they descended the stairs to the street, where they said their good-byes. Delgado shuffled away to join the crowd around the *presentador* and a trio of guitars.

Martin paused between two half-rusted cars. Lights hanging in front of the shops and clubs swayed in the gentle wind gliding up from the ocean, their rhythm illuminating the revelers, seemingly matching their beats. A few individuals had stumbled away, the late hour clearly beckoning them to their beds. With one last glance, Martin struck up a narrow street toward Hotel La Rusa a few blocks away.

Laughter rose behind him and he looked back. An American couple was locked in a playful embrace. The man backed the woman against the wall, a grin on his face, and she giggled. Coming up the street behind them, three men smiled and joked. The one in the middle staggered, and the other two caught him and held him up between them—the three men Martin had seen earlier outside the nightclub. *Don't jump to conclusions. It's a small town.*

The Panther of Baracoa

He veered right at the corner, away from the heart of the town. Shadows deepened. Heavy black electrical wires that stretched low between the houses hummed and pricked his hair on end. The narrow street was steeped in desertion.

Thirty meters behind Martin, footsteps on paving bricks cut through the night. He cocked his head to the side to see the three men with his peripheral vision. They were no longer laughing, and the "drunk" one was suddenly sober.

Martin's stomach knotted. A porch light ahead of him shut off. The street went black. Who had hired the men? FSB? DGI? The Dutch? Edurne had said he would no longer be safe in America. Had she been captured? Were they CIA? Or maybe it was the mob that would soon be losing its cheap cocoa source?

The footsteps behind him sped up. *They want to take me alive, or they would have fired already.*

Cold sweat broke out on Martin's neck. He swallowed hard and held his pace. He had enough of a lead to make it to the next corner. A black fog descended on his soul. That morning, he had been one predator among other known predators, each keeping to his own corner of the jungle— each happy with his place in the food chain. But now, some unknown stalker had invaded.

Edurne was right. There was no peace for him in Cuba. No cocoa plantation. No life of ease with the finest cigars and rum. No relief from the hellish reality of predator and prey. A cry went up inside him, and he quickly extinguished it. This was no time to whine about lost dreams.

Chapter Four

MARTIN CUT AROUND THE LAST CORNER TO LA RUSA and quickened his pace, debating his options. He strolled through the front door of the hotel and went to the bar. The young Dutch couple from the beach sat at a table along the wall, wine in their hands and their heads close together. Were they working with the bastards outside? They didn't glance up from their conversation, but professionals wouldn't.

Martin, wishing he'd picked up a pistol in *Habana* for his "low-risk assignment," settled at the end of the counter where he could easily grab a bottle from behind the bar to use as a weapon if needed. Back to the wall, he kept one eye on the Dutch couple and the other on the stairs going up to the rooms. Then he mustered a grin for the bartender. *"Santiago de Cuba, por favor."*

The bartender poured a shot of the rich, dark rum. "Did you enjoy our weekly festivities?"

Martin tipped back the rum but only sipped. "Jolly good party."

The Panther of Baracoa

Come on. Take the bait. Martin waited for the men outside to make their move.

A leggy redhead and her perky blonde friend approached the front desk. The redhead gave Martin a wink. He raised his glass to her and forced a slight smile.

Just then, the man who had pretended to be drunk appeared in the lobby.

Here we go. Martin turned back to the bartender. "I'll be climbing El Yunque tomorrow."

The man in the lobby scanned the area and headed up the stairs.

The bartender beamed. "You must talk to my cousin Juan. He has the best tours. He takes you . . ."

Martin pretended rapt attention as the bartender elaborated on the virtues of Juan's tours, giving the stalker time to reach Martin's third-floor room and let himself in. After two minutes, Martin stood and tossed a five-peso note on the counter. "Sounds like Juan has a great deal. Thanks for the tip."

"*Gracias,* señor."

Martin headed for the front door, not about to fall into the trap the three men had set for him by splitting up, positioning one of them in his room so two could box him in from behind. He paused and steeled himself. At least now the odds were only two to one.

He darted his gaze right and left, taking in everything, then exited the hotel. A slight motion in the shadows across the street registered in his peripheral vision. *There you are, you bastards. Not what you expected is it?*

A wave crashed against the seawall. The wind had picked up, and a squall was coming inland. A handful of pedestrians scattered along the sidewalks, and a few horse-drawn carts and bitaxis meandered past on the wide street,

BAYARD & HOLMES

their pace slowed to almost a crawl through the late-night hour. Martin turned sideways to the gusts and held himself to a measured stroll along the oceanfront, the two men slipping through the shadows behind him.

He spotted a corner shop and ducked inside. It was hardly more than a cupboard with tourist baubles, flip-flops, hats, snacks, and rudimentary medical supplies crammed in like an *I Spy* picture. He located a bottle of rubbing alcohol and gauze. The bored clerk rang him up without a second glance.

Martin handed him exact change in Cuban pesos. The man sighed and pointed to a tiny sign behind the register. *"Tienda de dólares,* señor." A "dollar store." Foreign currency only. Martin passed him the money in British pounds, took his bag with the alcohol and gauze, and didn't wait for the change.

He stopped outside in the shop's porch light, took out a cigar, and waited while a horse-drawn cart full of tourists passed. Then he lit his cigar and headed up Malecón toward the docks. The two men gained ground behind him.

Martin drew on the cigar just enough to keep it lit. He heard the footsteps getting closer before the sound was drowned out by a passing bitaxi, the couple inside arguing in German about one of them dancing with another man. Martin's pulse pounded, and he lengthened his stride. He couldn't let the men catch up to him before he had them where he wanted them.

Changing course, he led the men back into the center of the town. With one hand, he reached in the shop bag and tore open the box of gauze. His fingers met with close plastic wrapping around the roll. *Bloody hell.*

An old woman sat on her porch with a juicing machine and baskets of fruit next to her. She stared at Martin. Was

The Panther of Baracoa

she hoping for one more sale, or was she with them? Two bitaxis parked ahead at the side of the narrow street, their young drivers conversing and gesticulating with gusto.

Martin peeked sideways. His pursuers were only nine meters behind. He forced himself to relax and searched up the lane. He spotted a dark, narrow street just past the bitaxis. *There.* He hastened as much as he dared and ducked into it. Then he ripped the gauze package out of the bag and tore open the plastic.

The men followed him into the empty passage. Martin whipped out the alcohol, opened it, and shoved the gauze inside the top of the bottle. He shook it to wet the gauze, and he slowed his pace.

The footsteps drew closer. Martin's back itched between his shoulder blades, and he consciously slowed his heartbeat. Had he miscalculated? Would they simply shoot him in the back and be done with it now that they had him in a dark alley?

Hold... Four meters... *Hold*... Three meters... Two meters... *Now!*

Martin lit the gauze with the cherry of his cigar. He spun and hurled the flaming bottle into the chest of the man on his right. The plastic ruptured with the heat, and the fiery liquid engulfed the front of the man's torso. He twisted sideways, screaming.

His partner reached for a pistol in his belt. Martin leapt forward and caught his wrist before he could angle the gun around. Spinning parallel to the man, he yanked the thug's arm down hard toward the ground, throwing the man off balance. When the man recovered and straightened, Martin bent his elbow and shot him in the chest with his own gun.

The man dropped to his knees. Martin wrested the gun from the man's hand and put a second bullet through his head. Without pause Martin turned the pistol on the shrieking partner, his entire upper body now engulfed in flames, and ended the man's agony.

The bitaxi drivers appeared at the end of the street. Martin jumped back and then ran the opposite direction. When he reached the corner, he cut around it and slowed to a brisk walk.

A man dashed toward him. "What happened?"

"A bit too much alcohol, I think." Martin fought to keep his voice even.

The man seemed puzzled, squinting from Martin to the alleyway. Martin passed him and compelled himself to maintain a measured stride, heading toward the docks where the fishermen were securing their vessels and unloading their nets.

The first raindrops hit his face. He blinked away the light rain and assessed the boats. He chose one of the bigger ones and approached the man on board.

"*Hola,* señor." The man's eyes held curiosity but no fear.

Martin had no time for small talk. "I need immediate transport to the Dominican Republic."

The man stepped back. "You are mistaken. I am a simple fisherman, not a smuggler. Besides, there is a storm coming in. No one is going anywhere. Come back tomorrow. Perhaps my brother will help you."

Sirens sounded in the distance. Martin withdrew five hundred British pounds from his wallet. "I need immediate transport to the DR."

The fisherman raised his eyebrows. The sirens moving toward them grew louder. The man reached for the bills and pointed to the wheelhouse. "Hurry inside, my friend. I will take you to Florida in a *huracán* for this if you like."

"The DR will do nicely, thank you." Martin ducked

The Panther of Baracoa

into the cover, and the man untied the boat from its moorings. Soon they were underway.

Martin checked to make sure the USB drive was still secure in his pocket. *What are you?* He ran his thumb across it while he watched the shore receding in the rain. The cheerful tropical colors of the lit buildings taunted the bleak darkness churning inside him. What could be on the drive? Who was hunting him? And would he ever be able to return to Cuba?

Realizing he was about to lose signal, Martin took out his phone to check for any messages from MI6. He tapped in a series of counterintuitive camera settings to reveal an internal screen. The message there stopped him cold.

"Call me when you get the chance. I'll be at home. K. W."

Go immediately to K. W.—Quetta, Pakistan—and wait for contact.

Chapter Five

CARS, TRUCKS, AND BUSES BLARED THEIR HORNS AT THE donkeys, motorized rickshaws, and bicyclists while shoppers, vendors, and tourists elbowed their way through the impossible crush of traffic, conversing in Urdu, Pashto, English, and various Balochi dialects. Vivid placards sported slogans written in both English and Urdu, reflecting the increasing Western presence in the ancient city of Quetta. Their festive hues broke a sharp contrast to the one- and two-story gray buildings laced together with a vast weave of humming wires reminiscent of the Cuban town Martin had fled only three days before.

He paid the taxi driver in rupees and waited until the car was well away before he slung the laptop case containing clothing and toiletries over his shoulder. Then he headed up the busy street in Quetta's Hazara Town.

The smell of roasted corn from a street cart mingled with the spicy odor of lamb sajji, a regional dish. Martin followed his nose to a shop three doors up that sold it, along with fruit, computers, and locally made clothing. The scent merged with the waft of bread from the French bakery next

The Panther of Baracoa

to it, only to be overwhelmed by the ubiquitous dirt and car exhaust and the malodorous press of two million people. The stench hung as low and heavy as the gray autumn chill.

Martin wrinkled his nose and pulled his overcoat closer over the casual business suit he had picked up from a British tailor in Karachi. His mind flashed on the clean air and warm beaches of Cuba. He pushed the image away. This was his life now, not that, and this life had to be survived.

He shoved his hand in his pocket, and his fingers touched the USB drive. He clinched his teeth and shook his head. He had better things to worry about, like why MI6 had ordered him back when they had worked so hard to get him to Cuba. But first things first. He needed some firepower.

A ring tone by the popular Pakistani rock band Junoon rose above the chaos at his ten o'clock, and a bicyclist came to a hard stop beside Martin to answer the phone call. Martin tensed and studied the man's face. No one he knew, but that didn't mean much in a place where assassins were cheaper and more common than prostitutes, and prostitutes were cheaper and more common than baked bread.

Three blocks down, Martin entered a side street, which he followed for half a mile into a quieter part of the city. He heard the whizzing of an impact wrench and smelled the old grease emanating from three car bays well before he reached the mechanic's shop. He stepped inside, passed two men chatting in the waiting area, and went straight to the counter. A young clerk in a Quetta Gladiators ball cap and a work jumper was making entries in a computer. The name *Karim* was embroidered at his shoulder

"Hello, Karim. Is your father in?" Martin asked.

Karim looked up and nodded. "Good day, Mr. Collins. He is in his office."

"Thank you." Martin made his way past the end of the counter and up the hallway to where the second door on the right stood open. He knocked, and a bald, middle-aged man with a mustache glanced up from his computer and grinned. His jumpsuit with the embroidered name *Ahmad* was clean, but his fingernails were black from decades of working in his shop—the family business. Stacks of Mercedes, Toyota, and Honda manuals overflowed the table behind him, along with ledgers, pricing guides, and manila folders.

He stood and offered a hand. "Welcome, friend. I was wondering if the Tali-buggers had gotten you. May I offer you a spot of tea?" His fluent English was colored with a British accent.

Martin shook his hand. The fact that Pakistanis didn't hug him was the only silver lining of being called back from Cuba. "Thank you, no. Perhaps we could take a walk?"

Ahmad paused, and then he became all business. "Come with me. I will show you how my darling is blossoming."

Martin followed Ahmad down the hall and into a work yard where a few cars and a motorized rickshaw waited their turn for repairs. They headed to a garage with a single apricot tree at its corner. Ahmad unlocked the corrugated steel bay door and rolled it up. Inside sat a nearly completed classic Aston Martin, his prize project. It was a conglomeration of parts he'd acquired over the years from scrap and from pieces ordered off the internet.

Martin laughed. "You've got to have at least five different models here, but I'm sure if someone from Aston saw this, they would steal the design. She's beautiful!"

Ahmad beamed. "One of your British mates over at the Polo Club drank a bit too much after a match. As fortune

The Panther of Baracoa

would have it, he managed to spare the exact fender she needed when he crashed into his own house. Now, I'm only waiting for a carburetor."

"Congratulations," Martin said, meaning it. Ahmad had been working on the car since before Martin had met him four years earlier.

Ahmad grabbed a cloth from a shelf and polished away a speck of dust from the new fender. "You need a car, my friend?"

"No. I need a pistol and some ammo—nothing Chinese or Pakistani. It needs to work."

Ahmad raised an eyebrow but asked no questions. "You're in luck. I obtained some excellent ammo yesterday right off of the NATO shipment."

Luck, my arse, you old devil. Martin smiled. "If only the government were as efficient as your black market. What about a pistol?"

Ahmad paused, his gaze resting on a cabinet in the corner. "I do have one, but it's promised to an oil company chap who'll be arriving later this week."

"Later this week? Anything could fall off a NATO truck between now and then. Why not just show it to me?"

Ahmad's eyes twinkled. "No harm in showing you."

He gave the Aston one more stroke with the polishing cloth and crossed to the cabinet. He reached behind it to release a hidden lock and then eased out a rectangular box the size of a laptop computer case. He opened it to display a wooden-handled Browning Hi-Power 9mm and two extra fourteen-shot magazines. It all appeared to be in pristine condition.

Martin suppressed a grin. "You tested it?"

Ahmad nodded. "Last week. She's a prize. You can't

miss with this one—your bullets will travel like homing missiles."

Martin resisted the urge to laugh at Ahmad's exaggerations. "She's adequate, anyway. A thousand British for the pistol and a hundred rounds of ammo."

"The oil fellow would pay two thousand American."

"Their money's worth less all the time." Martin took out his cash, knowing the power of a bird in the hand. "Fifteen hundred British."

Ahmad eyed Martin's money a moment and then held out the box with the Browning. "It's true. You never know what will fall off a NATO truck between now and then." He stowed the British pounds with practiced ease.

Martin returned his wallet to his pocket, and his fingers brushed the USB drive. An idea came to mind. "Have you seen Roger Mantle lately?"

Ahmad nodded. "He came around last week."

A load lifted from Martin's shoulders. John the Yank—someone he knew he could trust. "Is he still in town?"

"I don't know. From the things he picked up, I would guess he was heading into the hills. But I can find out for you. Where can I get you a message?"

"Hasan Changezi's. The flats by the cemetery." With a back door to escape into the mountains.

"I'll send Karim to let you know what I find out about Mr. Mantle."

Martin loaded the Browning, stuck it in the back of his waistband, and stored the bag of ammo in the laptop case. Then he left Ahmad's warm welcome for the cold streets of the city.

Chapter Six

MARTIN STARED OUT THE SECOND-FLOOR WINDOW OF the flat. How did buildings in Quetta manage to become derelict before they were even finished being built? Brick-and-plaster hovels crept into the distance toward a tree-lined road that ran through a graveyard at the foot of the mountains. The fact that the graveyard was the most beautiful part of the city said everything.

Below him on the gray, earth-packed street, a toy vendor meandered past, obscured by his overflowing rack of blow-up Coca-Cola balls, farm animals, boats, and small balloon chairs. A little boy tugged the hand of a woman in a pink hijab and pointed to a balloon horse. She smiled and purchased it for the child, who hugged it to his chest, grinning as they continued down the street. Martin warmed at the sight.

"Very nice flat. You see?" Hasan Changezi swept his arm toward the view.

Martin drew the curtain closed and a corner sagged. He appraised the room. A serviceable brown chair with the barest hint of stuffing coming out the edge of the seat cushion squatted next to a small end table with a lamp—the only furniture in the living area. A few meters away, a metal-frame table and two straight-back chairs crowded the center of a tiny kitchen with a rust-stained sink, two pans, a patch of counter space, and a hot plate. He had already seen the double bed in the front room, and it was sound enough. No sign of vermin.

The cries of Hasan's youngest son drifted all the way up the stairwell. "I'd prefer something off the street," Martin said. "Perhaps my old place in the back by the stairwell?"

"So sorry. We rented that one out yesterday. There is only this one and one on the ground floor by the goat shed."

Martin pursed his lips and considered his options for quick exits. Too far for a dash down the stairs. The straight drop through the window to the busy street below could leave him injured and would make stealth nearly impossible. But ground floor by the goat shed? Bad juju all around. No one but Ahmad knew he was in town so far, so this second-floor room would do for tonight. Tomorrow, he would find someplace else and have this flat for a spare.

He went to the small loo and tested the shower. A stream sprinkled out of the showerhead, while a stout leak sprayed the surround. *Definitely find someplace else tomorrow.*

"For you, I give discount." Hasan quickly turned off the shower. "Only twenty-five thousand rupees."

The equivalent of one hundred and fifty pounds British. Thirty pounds more than it was worth. Martin took twenty thousand rupees from his wallet and held them up to Hasan without a word.

Hasan reached for the money. "Good to have you back, sir."

When the landlord was gone, Martin sat down at the

The Panther of Baracoa

kitchen table and dialed the number for MI6 on his mobile phone. A taped message picked up on the second ring, and a pleasant feminine computer voice greeted him. *"Thank you for phoning Cold Tarts Ice Cream. Your call is very important to us. For customer service . . ."*

Martin didn't wait for the tape to finish. He dialed in his code to reroute to Communications, looking forward to hearing the British voice of one of the team of women who moderated between MI6 and him. Then he could find out what the hell was going on, and how soon he could return to England.

A man spoke through the connection. "Hello."

Martin straightened in his chair. He didn't recognize the voice. "Who is this?"

"I'm Alastair. I'll be taking care of your coms for this operation." The impersonal nasal tones gave Martin an image of a consummate paper pusher.

He tensed. It wasn't unprecedented to have someone new handling the coms, but it was unusual. "Is Henrietta there?"

"I think Henrietta will be back soon. I'm not sure. You need to wait for her."

Martin sighed. Sit tight and wait for contact. Not the answer he wanted. "Thank you, Alastair." He put the phone back in his pocket and analyzed the pit in his stomach. He hated waiting blindly for orders in a foreign country where even the most benign outsiders were at risk, much less men of his own ilk. And why was he ordered back in the first place? Martin could not imagine the answer to that question. *Make the best of it.*

A knock at the door brought him back to the moment. He peered through the spyhole. Karim, still in his work

33

jumper. Surprised that he had an answer so soon, Martin opened the door. "Yes?"

"The car will be ready at six o'clock tonight. I can send it here, or you can pick it up at our shop."

John could come by at six, or Martin could meet him at Ahmad's. Martin smiled. "Brilliant. Please send it here. I look forward to its arrival."

Karim touched his hand to the brim of his cap and sauntered down the hallway.

Martin sat back down at the kitchen table and took out the USB drive. *Don't get too comfortable, you little troublemaker.*

Studying it in his hand, he reviewed his plan. He would pass it off to John as soon as possible, and John would get it to safety in the United Kingdom until Martin could return home himself and find out what was on it.

It would be good to see John. Good to see a friend.

Chapter Seven

RUM FLOWED THROUGH MARTIN'S DREAMS AS SPANISH guitars wove their sensual rhythms around Afro-Cuban drums and marimbas. A little brown girl with flowers in her hair took him by the hands and led him into the middle of the dancers on Calle Antonio Maceo.

He laughed and rocked with the beat. Then the little girl was gone, and Edurne was in her place, her beautiful black hair and inviting hips giving ethereal life to the music. She seized Martin's eyes with her own, and he felt himself falling.

She leaned in close. "Leave Cuba now, and never come back."

The guitars sped up to a frantic pace. The drummers lost the beat, and the marimbas competed in their discord. A doorknob jangled in the background.

A doorknob!

Shocked from his sleep, Martin flew up from the bed. He snatched the Browning. The wall clock showed 5:30 p.m. John wasn't due until 6:00, and no one else knew Martin was here.

The front door shattered at the lock and slammed in. Martin rounded out of the bedroom and fired once to the chest and once to the head. A Pakistani man crashed to the floor. Another two men behind him jumped and ran down the hall, their pistols in hand.

Martin shoved his feet in his shoes, stuffed his pockets with extra magazines and ammo, and crept to the doorway. He froze and listened. Nothing.

He lowered his head below where an assailant might expect to see it and peeked around the door frame. The resident from Martin's former flat came out with a large bag of rubbish and ambled toward Martin, whistling to whatever tune was playing through his earbuds connected to the iPhone in his shirt pocket.

The assailants were down the stairs, but Martin could still hear a voice. "Get up here, you idiots. He killed Mohammed."

Several voices answered with cries of *"Allahu Akbar."*

The neighbor, oblivious, stopped and beat his hand in the air four times as if on a drum before he continued toward the rubbish chute across from Martin's flat.

With the stairwell blocked, Martin was trapped. Chills crept up his spine. He forced himself to think. Shoot it out? No telling how many there were. Out the window? No. They'd have people in the street, even if he survived the drop.

Footsteps sounded in the stairwell. The neighbor opened the rubbish chute.

The rubbish chute!

Martin jammed the Browning in his waistband underneath his shirttail and pushed past the neighbor. The man startled back and dropped his bag. With a single motion, Martin propelled himself up off of the bag of rubbish and

The Panther of Baracoa

bounded into the chute feet first. Food scraps and ooze sucked onto his clothing as he plummeted toward the ground floor.

Something knocked off the side and fell into his eyes a moment before he shot out the bottom of the square tube into a bin full of bulging rubbish bags and debris. He landed hard.

Wiping his face clean, he heard footsteps running up the hall. He sprang from the bin, and a sharp pain stabbed up from his ankle. *Bloody hell!*

He limped to the back door that led onto the alley, unlocked it, and pushed the screen open. The hinges squeaked and he cringed. He assessed the distance to the street. Too far.

The voice from the stairwell sounded in the hallway. "Quick. The trash room." Footsteps pounded closer.

Leaving the alley door open to throw them off, Martin dove under the rubbish bags. He burrowed in among the rotting food, dirty diapers, and cigarette butts, and a sharp object stabbed him in the arm. The hallway door slammed open. He gulped in air and tasted ashes. It was all he could do not to sputter, but he held the breath, his body frozen.

The screen door hinges squeaked. "I don't see him."

The voice from the stairwell sounded, barely a meter away. "Split up. He can't have gone far."

The men spoke Urdu. Martin thought of an Urdu slave trader he had tangled with before he left Quetta. Did one of that bastard's people spot him? Even if they had, the slave trader had no reason to come for Martin now.

"Split up?" said the man by the door. "Are you crazy? He already killed Mohammed. I say we go back to the *gora* and tell him the man got away. We're not getting paid enough for this."

Gora? A white man?

Fear pricked at the nape of his neck. He raced through his memory. Did any Europeans want him dead? *That can't be right.* He'd have to sort it out later—if he survived.

The voice from the stairwell spoke again. "You knew who he was when we took the job and the money. We can't quit now."

Martin's lungs were near bursting. *Move on, you bloody bastards.*

A scuffle sounded from the door to the alley. More footsteps came in. "He didn't go south."

Martin heard the man from the stairwell move away from the rubbish bin. "You two go up and search the room. Look for any electronics. You two . . . come with me."

Electronics? The USB drive? . . . Don't. Breathe. Martin's insides squirmed, his body screaming for air.

Finally, he heard the screen door slam. Listening to the voices receding down the alley, he exhaled, surfaced above the debris, and gasped for air. Then he pushed over the edge of the bin, landing light on his feet. The ankle almost gave way. He fought back fear and pain.

Blood drenched his right sleeve from a piece of broken mirror stuck into his bicep. He braced and teased the razor-sharp shard from his arm. Blood flowed, seeping down his shirtsleeve.

Martin cut his sleeve at the shoulder seam with the mirror fragment and ripped it off. Using his left hand and his teeth, he tied off the wound with the ruined sleeve. Then he sliced the outside door screen half a meter above the ground and edged out the mirror in time to see the reflection of two men leaving the alley.

Martin waited a count of three and hurried the opposite direction, pistol in hand, his ankle shooting pain with each

The Panther of Baracoa

step. When he reached the corner, he stopped, crouched, and peeked around the building with the mirror.

A block up the street beside a dark sedan, Lewis Cambridge, the new station chief, stood staring at the front of the flats in the fading daylight.

Lewis the Prig? . . . MI6? . . . Martin's blood ran cold.

MI6 was trying to kill him.

Chapter Eight

MARTIN'S HEARTBEAT POUNDED IN HIS EARS. *KEEP YOUR head, man. This has to be a mistake.*

The two thugs who had run from his doorway crossed the road toward Lewis's car, pointing back toward the flats.

He had to get out of here.

Martin surveyed the street. A few lights already shone through windows. The kebab shop was shutting its doors, street vendors were packing up their wares, and fruit stands were closing for the day. Could he hide in one of their booths? No chance.

The balloon vendor he'd seen earlier entered the street at the end of the block, barely visible beneath the cascade of blow-up balls and farm animals that swayed from the tall rack he carried on his shoulders. Martin smiled grimly. He tucked his Browning into his back waistband and untucked his shirt to hide it. Then he took ten thousand rupees from his pocket and waited for the vendor to get closer.

He checked again around the corner with the mirror. The two men were arguing with Lewis. Lewis shook his head and signaled them to follow, starting toward the flats.

The Panther of Baracoa

Martin sought the balloon vendor once more. The man was halfway up the street, still coming toward him, his head partially obscured by the cows and boats. Martin caught the vendor's eye, put his finger to his lips, and held up the money.

The man looked right and left and then kept his eyes straight ahead, not even glancing at Martin. *Did he see me? Is he working for Lewis?* Martin fought off the urge to run. The vendor held a steady pace.

Martin didn't dare peek around the corner again. Lewis would know to watch for exactly that. When the vendor reached the edge of the alley, Martin once more showed him the money and indicated silence. The toy seller did not seem to notice but instead walked past him.

Martin's stomach lurched. *Now what?*

Then he heard a voice. "Come quickly."

Just then, two of the Pakistanis appeared at the far end of the alley. Martin rolled around the corner and leapt up. The toy vendor had already rotated his mountainous rack, shielding Martin from the view up the street.

Martin dove into the hanging toys. He passed the seller the money, and the man passed him the long stick that held up the contraption. Then the vendor stepped out from under his wares and walked back the way he had come, past the alley, and up the street.

Martin, under the wall of blow-up cows, horses, balls, and boats, crossed the road and headed up the block away from the flats, toward the center of Hazara Town.

By the time he reached a bazaar two blocks away, his ankle was screaming in pain. He didn't slow down. Though it wasn't likely, the balloon vendor could just as well make another ten thousand rupees from Lewis by selling him information. Martin needed distance. A bus came toward him from up the street.

A girl's voice sounded outside the wall of toys. "Mommy, auntie, see the cow?" Two haggard-looking women in blue hijabs with five children between them caught up to the girl.

One of the women took the child's hand. "Not today. We have no money for toys."

Martin stuck his head out of the mound. "It's all yours." He leaned the rack against the wall of a shop and took down a cow. He gave it to the little girl and spoke to the mother in Urdu. "Take the whole rack. It's yours."

The mother wrinkled her brow, clearly skeptical. Martin limped away without checking to see if she took him at his word.

A bicyclist veered Martin's direction. Martin moved his hand closer to his pistol and skirted around a child selling the last of the bread in a basket. A group of women stopped and stared at him. Martin glanced down at his arm where fresh blood trickled out from under the makeshift bandage. The bright blue-and-green city bus was a block away on the opposite side, but its next stop was directly across from him.

A pickup full of bleating sheep made a U-turn in the street and parked in front of a sajji restaurant to make a live animal delivery. The driver and his passenger hopped out. One climbed into the truck bed, scooped up a sheep, and handed it down to the other man over the top of the wooden side slats. Then the man in the truck bed jumped down and returned to the passenger seat while the man holding the sheep approached the restaurant.

While they were distracted, Martin dropped his phone between the slats into the back of the truck. Then he entered the street and wove through traffic to the opposite

The Panther of Baracoa

side. The bus stopped at the curb, and he jumped on it, not caring where it was going. Anywhere was better than here.

The bus was packed with people heading home after the workday. Martin pushed his way to one of the last two seats open in the back. He sat quickly and slouched low while the bus driver gabbed with a man on the sidewalk, apparently forgetting about his duties.

A block away, Lewis's thugs rounded the corner. Had the vendor sold Martin out? Sweat beaded on his forehead.

The thugs searched the emptying bazaar, their gazes passing over the balloon rack where children and parents were filling their arms with toys. Then one of the thugs pointed toward the truckload of sheep.

Bollocks! The phone . . . Move this bloody bus!

The bus driver gestured with his hands and raised his voice at the man on the sidewalk. Martin couldn't quite catch his words, but his tone was passionate.

Lewis's Pakistanis ran ahead of him, their guns out, toward the sheep. One of them fired into the pickup bed. A man ran out of a shop three doors down and fired at the shooter. Another of Lewis's thugs joined in. Bullets went wild. People screamed and ran.

The shepherd in the passenger seat leapt out, his eyes wide with horror, watching the assassin slaughter his meager livelihood. The animals crowded in panic, rocking the truck. The shooter killed one sheep and then another. Blood sprayed from between the wooden slats. The shepherd fell to his knees, his palms pressed together, begging the criminal to stop.

One of the remaining sheep leapt on top of another and over the side of the enclosure. Frenzied with terror, it rocketed directly toward the shooter. Its hooves landed on the assailant's chest and knocked him to the ground. The man's pistol flew into the air, and his head cracked on the cement curb. His body went limp. Blood seeped across the sidewalk.

Two more sheep followed, stomping him under their hooves and running down the street. The shepherd gave chase, waving his arms in despair. The other thugs fired after him. The man dropped in front of a car. The car swerved around his body and sped away.

The bus driver slammed the doors shut and stomped on the gas. The last Martin saw of his pursuers was Lewis yelling and gesturing frantically at his hired thugs, while the last sheep leapt from the pickup and trampled the assassin's body.

Two blocks away, Martin released a breath he didn't realize he was holding. Glancing around the bus to study his fellow occupants, he noticed a man and his wife across the aisle from him. They sat up, having ducked down when the shooting started. They both stared at Martin's arm.

"Are you okay?" the man asked. "Did you get robbed?"

Martin assessed them. Business suit, fluent English, well-dressed wife. Perhaps a criminal, but not one trying to kill him. The young wife bowed her head and shyly peeked up at Martin from under her brown hijab.

"Yes, but all they got was my phone."

The man's brow wrinkled, and his voice held genuine concern. "Was it a Sunni Muslim gang? You know they are savages."

"No, no. Just common rubbish."

The man offered a clean handkerchief from his jacket pocket. "I can help you with your bandage."

Martin paused the briefest moment and then held out his arm. "Thank you." The man covered Martin's bloody makeshift bandage with the handkerchief and tied it off.

The Panther of Baracoa

The bus slowed to a stop, and the stranger said, "This is where we get out. Would you like to come with us? My brother knows a doctor."

"Thank you, no. That's very kind of you, but I'm meeting up with a friend who can stitch it for me."

The man and his wife stood. "Then farewell, and be careful. You are not in England anymore."

Bloody hell, you think?

Martin nodded to the couple. "Thank you."

Chapter Nine

THE LIGHTS OF THE CITY PASSED BY OUTSIDE THE BUS window. Martin's ankle throbbed and facts tumbled in his head, refusing to coalesce into a coherent picture. MI6 had fought for months to get him out of Pakistan and into Cuba. At least now he knew why they had ordered him back to Pakistan. He smiled grimly to himself. Much easier to kill him inconspicuously here than it would have been on the island. In Cuba, he was the honored guest from the UK Department of Business Innovation and Skills. There, he would have been missed. Here, he would only be another dead body among faceless scores.

But why kill him at all? Assassinating your own was popular in films but rarer than an honest politician in the field. It had to have something to do with the USB drive—that was the only thing that had changed, and Lewis's thugs were specifically searching for electronics. What could possibly be on it?

In the past Lewis had expressed concerns to their superiors about Martin's drinking and underworld friends, but

The Panther of Baracoa

Martin had laughed, putting it off to the man's class prejudices. Was this a personal vendetta?

No. Lewis was a prig, but he was a good agent and a loyal Englishman to the core. He had to be following orders, but whose? And what was their agenda? Martin had to get the USB to safety until he could see what was on it.

He shifted, trying to get comfortable, but his leg was in agony. He needed help. He couldn't go to anyone in MI6 until he knew what was happening. John would be at Martin's flat by now. Lewis would have left someone there to watch who would surely report on the unknown American. Martin couldn't risk blowing John's cover to MI6 or making him a target by attempting to contact him again.

Martin considered contacting his own men—that army of friends outside of intelligence channels that every deep-cover agent cultivated ... No. He didn't want to expose them. Besides, if MI6 was after him, everyone in the shadow world would be targeting a six-foot blond, blue-eyed Englishman. He needed someone completely above suspicion and above the reach of the street—someone completely removed from that existence.

Only one person came to mind, but would she want to see him? He'd asked her to come with him to the Caribbean, offering to settle her in the Dominican Republic. She'd refused, unwilling to leave her medical practice. He could hardly blame her for that, especially since he hadn't asked her to marry him. But had she moved on? Would she welcome his call?

Martin rode the bus for forty-five minutes while more and more people emptied out and the night set in. When it finally stopped outside of Hazara Town, he stepped onto the sidewalk. Favoring his ankle, he eased across the narrow, empty street toward an open corner shop selling dried fruit, phones, tobacco, candy, and hats. He took a prepaid mobile phone and some fruit up to the counter.

The middle-aged clerk spotted his bloody bandage and disheveled state and eyed him with suspicion. "What happened to you?"

"Just a small scuffle."

"It was Hazaras, wasn't it?" The man spit on the ground. "Those Shiite Hazaras are savages."

"No. They weren't Hazaras."

"Humph. It would have been. If you have any self-respect at all, stay out of Hazara Town."

Martin paid for the phone and fruit. "Could you please call me a cab, or do you know someone who would like to make a few rupees?"

The man shifted uncomfortably and glanced toward the door behind Martin. "Just you?"

"Just me."

"Do you have any packages?"

"No." Martin eased more weight off his ankle, eager to get to safety. He understood the man's hesitance and questions. Bombings were common throughout the city, and the clerk clearly didn't want to be a part of one.

"Where are you going? Do you need a doctor?"

"Samungli Road. I'm meeting a friend who will take care of me." As if for emphasis, a trickle of blood escaped the bandage and traced down his arm.

The clerk handed him a handful of tissue from under the counter. "Three thousand."

"Two thousand. That's five hundred more than a cab would cost."

"Twenty-five hundred. I'm having a slow night, or I would not take you at all."

Martin nodded and handed the clerk the money. The

The Panther of Baracoa

man closed the front door of his shop and led Martin out back to his ancient Toyota.

———

Thirty minutes later, Martin stood on the street a block away from Benazir Park at the edge of Jinnah Town. He waited until the shop owner drove away before he hobbled up the road that ran alongside the park toward a graveyard, clinching against his pain and willing his ankle not to give out. The night chill sank into his bones. He popped the battery into the prepaid phone and dialed.

Three rings. *Please answer.* Was she working late at the hospital? Did she have a date? It rang four more times. Finally, a woman came on the line. "Hello?"

At the sound of her lilting voice, a lump formed in Martin's throat. He paused.

"Who is this?"

He swallowed. "Hello, Farah. It's Martin."

"Martin? Martin! It's good to hear from you. Are you in Canada?"

He warmed to hear the welcome in her voice. He didn't know what was still there for him, but Martin was glad to know something was. "No. Actually, I'm at a graveyard near Samungli Road. Care for some company? I need your help." He reached a tombstone and sat down. The cold concrete bit through his trousers, and he shivered. "Can you come pick me up? I'll explain when I see you."

She hesitated. Martin's heart froze. Was he wrong to call?

"Have you been in town long?"

"No. I got here today."

When she spoke again, she sounded relieved. "Where shall I come for you?"

"I'm behind Benazir Park where it meets the back of the Hudda Graveyard. Pull up from Samungli Road and park, and I'll slip into your backseat."

"The backseat? What? Are you in trouble?"

The confusion in her voice evoked a pang of guilt. "There are people looking for me. I'll explain when I see you."

"I'm on my way. And Martin . . . I'm glad you called *me*."

He smiled at the emphasis she put on the last word. The circumstances were hardly the best, but it would be good to see her.

Chapter Ten

FARAH'S HONDA CIVIC STOPPED AT THE CURB. STAYING low, Martin slipped from the shadows. He opened the back door, slid inside, and lay low across the seat as he pulled the door shut. "Keep driving." He felt the car roll forward.

"What kind of trouble are you in?" She frowned, her eyes on the road.

Martin shifted to keep his bleeding arm off her upholstery. "I quite honestly don't know."

"Why aren't you in Canada? Or the Caribbean?"

"Well, I owe it to you at this point to tell you . . . I'm not a Canadian geologist."

She snorted. "I rather figured that out. So are you one of those opium smugglers? Because if you are . . ."

"No. Nothing like that." The car turned right. Martin's ankle throbbed, and he grunted. "I work for a foreign government, but I don't work against Pakistan or against the UK."

"I see." Her voice was tense. "So you must work for British Secret Service."

"Not exactly."

"That means 'exactly,' doesn't it? You're a spy."

Martin cringed at the word. Spying was something seedy . . . something the Russians and Israelis did. "I prefer the term *intelligence specialist*." He waited for her response, but none came.

Did I say too much? An uncomfortable feeling began to grow. *Perhaps this is a bad idea.*

Finally, she said, "I suppose I can understand why you wouldn't be up front with that right off, but now's your chance. Is there anything else you need to come clean about? Because I won't tolerate dishonesty. It's all right if you say you can't tell me, but don't tell me lies."

Martin considered the things he had told her about himself during their eight months together, and he chose his words carefully. "I play polo, and I love horses. I love the outdoors. I hate opera, I love to cook, and I love to draw pictures in the sketchpad you gave me. Everything you know about who I am is true. As for what I do, I can't say any more at this time. But you know the real me, Farah. You know *me*."

This time, the silence lasted longer. Martin waited, mentally reviewing his options should she reject him. Who else could he turn to? No one who would be safe if he did. Perhaps he could steal a car and run?

"And is Martin Collins your real name?"

He hesitated. Once spoken, he could never unspeak it, but she was his best hope, and he owed her what truth he could give her. "Well . . . no. My name is Martin Wentworth Blackburn."

"Should I know that name?"

"No." No one should. Though his mother was a baroness, she was wealthy enough to keep the family in the shadows. "We're not important outside of certain circles."

The Panther of Baracoa

A horn blared, and Farah swerved hard to the left, laying on her own horn in return. "Bloody tosser!"

Martin leaned up and peeked out the side window, his hand on his pistol. A gold Mercedes-Benz sports car was cutting across their lane to shoot into a parking complex.

Farah shook her head. "Cheeky bugger just moved in down the hall. This isn't the first time he's done that to me."

I'd like to make certain that it's the last.

Martin ducked back down, and she angled into a parking garage. He felt the spiraling curves as she drove to the fifth floor of her ten-story building and parked. He peeked out the window again. A dim light glowed beside a closed-circuit camera between a lift and a doorway twelve meters away.

"Would you like one of my scarfs to put over your face?"

She was going to let him stay. The tight feeling in his throat relaxed. "No. That would cause suspicion. I'll walk in with you, and with any luck, security will be asleep or busy in some porn chat room."

Martin turned his head toward her and saw her face for the first time in weeks. He caught his breath. Her amber eyes were even more beautiful than he remembered. Tendrils of long, dark-brown hair had escaped her ponytail and framed the strong angles of her olive-toned face. His gaze held hers, and she smiled. "I don't know what brought you back, Martin, but I'm glad you're here."

He returned her smile. "Let's get inside, and I'll tell you what I can." He got out of the car and opened her door.

"You're limping. Can you walk?" She scrutinized him, and her eyebrows drew together. "And how bad is that wound under the bandage?" She pointed to his arm.

"I'll be fine, Dr. Zaman." Martin took a step and winced.

Farah slid her shoulder under his arm. At five foot six, she was just tall enough to provide him comfortable support. "Lean on me."

"Never," Martin said, but as she steered him toward the door, he could not deny that she was helpful. "Well, all right. But only this once." He shifted to keep the blood-soaked bandage away from her coat.

Farah laughed. "Even now, you're too bloody proud."

"Maybe." He tried to smile, but it came out a grimace. Martin kept his face down while they approached the camera above the doorway. Farah swiped her key card, and they entered the building.

Once inside Farah's flat, Martin collapsed into an over-stuffed recliner and groaned with pain. The two-bedroom was spacious, with marble floors, ornate cabinets, and well-appointed furniture that evidenced her upper-middle class British roots. Like her father before her, along with one of her two older brothers, she had earned her medical degree at Leeds. Unlike them, she had returned to the land of her aunts, uncles, and cousins to practice her profession.

Martin glanced up at a picture of her that hung on the wall—a pencil sketch he had drawn of her passing out *halwa* pudding decorated with silver leaves to children at the orphanage where she volunteered when she wasn't working in the emergency room at Baseer Alim Hospital. Her idealism resonated with his, and studying the picture, he was again drawn to her pure and generous spirit—so different from the scumbags that populated the shadow world. She didn't know it, but he had contributed to that orphanage anonymously since he found out about her connection.

Farah closed the curtains, shutting out the view of the Quetta lights that stretched across the valley and up the

The Panther of Baracoa

hillside to the west. Then she knelt and unlaced Martin's shoe before coaxing it off his swollen foot.

He gritted his teeth. "I'll get the sock." He eased it back to reveal an engorged ankle where red, black, and blue competed for space across taut skin.

Farah didn't bat an eye. She tipped a reading lamp beside the chair to provide more light and inspected the joint a moment before she took his foot in her hands and gently rotated it. "Does this hurt?"

"Yes."

"And here?" She palpated the area.

"Yes, but mostly below the tibia."

"I'm not positive, but I think it's a bad sprain. We should get you to the hospital for an X-ray to be certain nothing is broken. You may have torn something, too. We don't have an MRI at Mercy, but I have a friend at the Military Hospital who might sneak you in for the right price."

"No!" Martin swallowed. "I mean, no. People are looking for me."

Her face solemn, Farah gazed up at him. "I'll ask you again. What kind of trouble are you in?"

Martin reached out a finger and stroked her cheek. "Some people I know are trying to kill me."

She paled and her eyes grew wide. Then she squared her shoulders and steadied herself. "I suppose this can't be too unusual in your line of work. We are in Pakistan, after all." She paused. "Will they want to kill me now, too?"

"No. I never told them about you. Not anyone. I would never let that world touch you." It wasn't only his missions he protected by keeping his private relationships to himself. "It has to be some kind of mistake that will properly sort out in time. I have no idea why they're after me, but it has something to do with this USB drive." He fished the blue bar from his pocket. "I don't even know what's on it. May I borrow your computer?"

"Yes, but first things first. You're bleeding." She pointed to his arm, where a bit of fresh blood brightened the kerchief. "And you need a bath. Sorry, love, but you smell like a dead goat rolled in a midden heap. Let's get you to the loo and mend you. Then you can clean up while I cook you some dinner and put together some ice packs. There'll be time after that to use the computer." She stood and moved to his side.

Martin caught her hand. "Farah . . . Thank you for your help. You know you owe me nothing."

Her eyes held Martin's, and he could not decipher the emotions in them. She patted his hand. "First things first."

Chapter Eleven

TEN STITCHES, ONE HOT BATH, THREE KEBABS, AND TWO ice packs later, Martin was once again stretched out in the recliner with his feet up. He drank in the comfort of his thick bathrobe—the one he had forgotten when he left for Cuba. It felt all the warmer because she had kept it in spite of their parting. She had refused to come with him, so why hadn't she gotten rid of it and moved on?

Farah handed him a cup of tea and her laptop and discreetly settled on a couch where she couldn't see the screen. Her face drawn tight, she sipped her own tea and looked across at him. Without a word, she took a ball of red yarn, a half-finished sweater, and knitting needles from a basket beside her and set her hands to work. Martin loved her domesticity—so different from the hard-nosed business-woman his mother was.

A rush of affection warmed him, and he smiled. Any other woman would go ballistic after what he'd told her, but she wasn't any other woman. She glanced up, and his gaze shot back to the computer.

Martin inserted the USB drive and retrieved the sole

file. As Edurne had said, photos of the beaches of Baracoa filled the screen. He felt a touch of longing and swiftly squelched it.

He tried several different ways to break into the encrypted information, and all failed. In fact, if Edurne hadn't told him the next layer was there, he would not have guessed. *Good.* It would be hard for someone else to guess, too.

Martin tumbled the problem over in his mind, thinking about the things Edurne had said. Whatever was on that drive, it involved Mexico, the United States, Russia, and possibly countries in Europe—all of the places she said he would not be safe again. Taken individually, each of those areas and governments posed unique issues and threats. Taken together, they simply made for strange bedfellows. And what plot could be so dangerous to so many?

Was it even MI6 that was trying to kill him or only Lewis? Lewis wasn't a lone player, but someone who knew about his background could work him with his class prejudices. It was possible someone outside of normal channels was behind it all. That would explain why Lewis was only using Pakistanis instead of MI6 agents. But who would do that, and why?

There was no way of knowing without the decryption codes. Percival would have picked them up two days before. Martin only had to secure the drive until he could decode it. Absently, he turned the family ring back and forth on his pinky while he pictured a map of Pakistan. Then he stopped and looked down at his hand, and a plan began to take shape.

MI6 may get me, but at least I can save the mission.

"Farah, do you have another USB drive around? Prefer-

The Panther of Baracoa

ably one like this." He pointed to the blue bar in the computer.

She set aside her knitting. "Yes, I think so." She rummaged through a rolltop secretary desk at the side of the room and then crossed over to him and held up a blue USB drive.

"Brilliant. Now how about those pictures of yours from the Dominican Republic you showed me from your trip last spring?"

"They're in the computer. May I step around and show you?"

Martin considered a moment. There was nothing perceptible in the tropical photos that could be classified, so seeing them most likely wouldn't put her at risk. "Please do. I could use your help with this."

Farah moved a chair beside Martin's recliner and leaned over to see the screen. "That's beautiful."

Martin smelled her familiar scent, and heat seared through his veins. "It certainly is." *First things first.*

She glanced up at him with a shy smile, then returned to the screen. "Is that where you were?"

Martin thought about what she had said in the car. No lies. "I'm not comfortable commenting on that . . . I need to make a decoy. If it's all right with you, I'd like to use some of your pictures from the DR."

"And then what?"

Martin inserted Farah's drive. "Then I'll have to get to Karachi unseen and send the original out of the country. Once it's away, I'll return to Quetta and let them see me sending off the copy. They'll intercept it, and decrypting it will keep them occupied long enough to allow the original to get to safety."

BAYARD & HOLMES

Farah scowled. "I'll come with you to Karachi. They won't be searching for a couple. You'll be safer with me."

"But you won't be safer with me. It's out of the question."

Farah stared at him, the same determination on her face that he had seen so often on his mother's. "Then I will take the USB drive to Karachi alone."

"No. I don't want you involved in this."

"I'm already involved, and you can't deny that it's a good idea. Do any of these people trying to kill you even know about me? No. You said so yourself, and I'm sure it's true or you wouldn't be sitting in my chair right now. Give me a head start, and then you mail the decoy and get away. They will never suspect that the real one is safe back in the UK." She stopped talking and waited.

Martin shifted uncomfortably in the chair. "But what about your patients? Don't you go to the emergency room or the orphanage tomorrow?"

"It's my day off at Baseer Alim, and there's a new doctor who visits the orphanage, so it's not only me now. Tomorrow is my day off there, too. See? I'm meant to do this for you. They'll never know to look for me."

Martin thought of the danger to her, and his throat constricted. She had been his refuge from that world since the day she had surprised him sitting alone before dawn in the gazebo on the island in Hanna Lake. He had started to stand, and she stilled him with a finger to her lips. Then she pointed to a hawk floating toward them. They froze in place until it passed, and then they watched the sunrise together in silence. After, when she spoke, her quick wit delighted his imagination, and her wise spirit calmed his soul, but it was her eyes that entangled his heart.

The Panther of Baracoa

From the start, she was precious and innocent, and he had kept a steel wall between her and the evil of his other world. He hated opening a crack in that wall, but she was right. They would never know to look for her. She would be safe enough taking the drive to Karachi as long as no one saw them together, and it was a good idea to have the original far from the decoy.

"All right. I think it can work, but if anyone sees you or if you suspect at any time you're being followed, get rid of it. I don't care what you do with it—just don't let them see you do it. Don't be caught with this or anything else connected to me."

Farah smiled. "It's a smart man who listens to a woman."

Martin chuckled. "It's a smart man who listens to you. Now I need you to pick up a few things from the corner shop for me. A six pack of cola—cans, not bottles—six large boxes of matches, waxed paper, duct tape, and sugar, and I'll need to use a pair of pliers while you're gone."

She raised an eyebrow. "What? You're going to drink cola and eat sugar while burning waxed paper and duct tape? As a doctor, I can tell you that none of those is good for you."

He grinned. "You guessed it. I've developed a fiendish cola and sugar addiction."

"If you say so." Farah began to stand up and then stopped. She glanced at Martin and then lowered her eyes. "You know, if you like, once you've mailed the decoy, you can come back here and stay with me."

Martin took her hand in his and caressed it. "No."

She nodded, still staring at the floor. "Then perhaps I could come with you?" She peered up at him and held his gaze. "I didn't know what you had come to mean to me until

61

you were gone. Perhaps . . . perhaps this is a chance to set things right. If you still want me, that is."

Hope shone in her eyes. Sadness crept through Martin. He drew her onto his lap and pressed a soft kiss to her lips. "Under different circumstances, that would make me the happiest man in the world, but what I want is not what matters now. These people who are trying to kill me . . . and they aren't only here in Quetta . . . they'll be watching for me everywhere. It simply wouldn't be safe for you to be with me now."

"But that's just it. They'll be watching for you. Not for a couple . . ."

"No."

She fell silent a moment. When she spoke again, her voice was soft and strained. "Then if you ask it, I'll wait for you."

Martin's heart swelled. He cradled her head in his hands and captured her mouth with a hungry kiss, hating what he had to say next. "It's not fair to ask you to wait—I might not survive this."

"Fair is a weather condition."

"It has to be your choice. I won't ask it. But if you do choose to wait for me, when I see you next, I'll bring you a ring."

Chapter Twelve

EIGHT HOURS LATER, MARTIN STOOD WITH FARAH AT her doorway. He wore brown salwar trousers and kameez tunic, a long chocolate wool vest, and a white turban typical of Baluchistan. He held a prayer rug under his arm, and a backpack full of his Western clothes rested on his shoulders. By the time she'd returned from the corner shop the night before, he had loaded her landscape pictures of the Dominican Republic onto the decoy drive and emptied fifteen of his 9mm shells of their gunpowder.

Farah helped him grind the match heads and mix them with the gunpowder and sugar to rub into layers of waxed paper and wrap inside three of the cola cans. They wrapped the loaded cans in duct tape to keep them from splitting apart once they were lit. Then they drank the other three sodas and reviewed their plan. Once everything was ready, Martin took her in his arms, and they made love through the night, full with the harsh reality that they might never meet again.

Now at the door, Martin set down the prayer rug and held her close. "I don't know how long I'll be away."

63

Farah nodded, her head against his chest. "I know . . . Isn't there anyone who can help you?"

Martin thought a minute. "There is a man who is here in Quetta often. An American. He goes by the name of Roger Mantle, but he's sometimes called John Viera. He's taller than me by about five centimeters. Tanned skin, reddish-brown hair, built about the same. His favorite saying is 'Every situation is improved by chocolate.' We met when he was saving my life. If you do happen across him, you can trust him with everything, but make sure it's him first."

"Roger Mantle, perhaps called John Viera, American, 'every situation is improved by chocolate.' Got it."

"Good girl." He gave her a brief kiss, not wanting to start something he didn't have time to finish. "You need to go now."

She gazed up at him, her eyes glistening. Then she opened the door and was gone.

Martin waited to give her a ten-minute head start, a lump forming in his throat. *Pull yourself together, man. You've got something to live for now.*

He closed his eyes and shut down his feelings, focusing his mind. When he opened them again, he was all business. *Let them see me mail the decoy and then disappear.* He left her world and locked the door behind him.

Remembering the asshole that had cut off Farah getting into the parking garage, Martin made a beeline for the gold Mercedes. He checked his watch. Four o'clock in the morning. She should be in Karachi by noon at the latest. Until then, he needed to be far away from her home in case he was spotted.

Martin picked the lock on the car door, tossed in the prayer rug and backpack, and slipped into the driver's seat.

The Panther of Baracoa

He popped out the ignition with a screwdriver and hot-wired the car. From the sound of the engine, it had recently had a tune-up. He shifted into gear and then drove out of the garage toward Hanna Lake to wait until he received Farah's text telling him she had succeeded.

Then it would be time to plant the decoy.

———

Eleven hours later, Martin wove through the center of Quetta, where the streets were wider and the buildings were one and two stories taller than in Hazara Town. Whitewash and broad windows prevailed over the ash grays and neon brights of the poorer areas. He steered the Mercedes into the car park of Radio Pakistan behind the Zehri Mosque and slipped between the bright white-and-tan buildings toward the FedEx at Swiss Plaza. Lewis was sure to have surveillance on the location since it was the only FedEx in the city. Martin was counting on it.

Half an hour earlier, Farah's text had arrived. "Uncle Bob will arrive on Tuesday." Now he had to take the last crucial step. He had to make sure MI6 intercepted the decoy without intercepting him. His ankle, though better after Farah's care and some rest, still ached, and not to limp while he carried the prayer rug under his arm was agony. Would he be able to get away? Martin willed himself to calm down.

He rounded the corner and blended into the crowd of men carrying their prayer rugs toward Jinnah Road. Already people were beginning to block the street. He had barely enough time to send the envelope and be off before the afternoon Dhuhr prayers brought the area to a halt.

Martin quickened his pace as best he could, studying

65

the people around him on the street, paying close attention to any Pakistani men who were focused on the crowd rather than on their own business. *I know you're here, you bloody bastards, but where are you?*

He scanned the area, his mind on a razor's edge. Apart from the crowd gravitating toward the Zehri Mosque, one man stood on a side street, casually glancing through the mass of people. Martin forced his body to relax. Two more men joined the first, and they proceeded down the side street in the opposite direction.

Come on, Lewis. Surely you thought to cover the FedEx. Frustration building, Martin kept moving. If he wasn't seen, his efforts would be wasted.

The modern, six-story concrete and glass of the Swiss Plaza rose in front of him, like something right out of the London or DC suburbs—clothing shops, an internet café, and gift shops on the street, with five upper floors of corporate offices. Martin ignored the pastries in the bakery window and spotted the FedEx, but instead of going in, he kept walking toward a blue arrow-shaped obelisk at the corner.

That's when Martin saw him—a man wearing a green jacket over his kameez, striding toward Swiss Plaza on Jinnah Road, looking at Martin without seeming to look.

Hook set. About three minutes now.

Martin ducked into the FedEx, where there was one customer leaving the counter and no others in the shop. *Perfect.* The imam began the call to prayer at the Zehri Mosque next door and Martin stepped forward, placing the envelope on the counter. "Please get this . . ."

The clerk held up his hand to cut Martin off and shook his head. Then he walked out from behind the counter, waving in the general direction of the mosque. Sorting

The Panther of Baracoa

through his key ring, he singled one out and locked the front door, preventing any more customers from entering during the service.

Martin glanced out the window and saw the man in the green jacket joined by another thug. The man in green gestured toward the FedEx and put his hand in his pocket. A pistol. The two of them began crossing the street.

I'm too late.

The clerk returned to the counter. Martin's pulse raced. He took three thousand rupees and a slip of paper from his wallet and set them beside the envelope. "Here's the address. Get that on the next truck and keep the change."

Glancing over his shoulder, Martin saw the men reach the curb, their glares staring him down. The man in green drew his pistol.

Martin hurdled the counter between himself and the clerk and landed hard on his one good leg. He bolted for the back room and located the door. Before he could reach it, bullets shattered the front glass and the clerk shouted. Martin dodged into a hallway. Adrenaline overriding his pain, he made for the exit at the back of the building.

He ran out into the narrow street between the Swiss Plaza and the Zehri Mosque and found his way blocked to the left by prostrate worshippers. Running to the right, he stumbled. After catching himself on a parked car, he made a limping dash for the end of the building.

A bullet exploded into the windscreen of a van parked in front of him. Martin staggered around the corner into an open lot that led back to Hali Road. Too far.

Martin spotted a large conifer tree at the edge of the lot and bounded behind it. He drew his pistol and waited. Soon, the man in the green jacket appeared level with him in the street and stopped. Was the other one with him? The

67

man in green squatted low, his pistol out, searching for Martin.

Martin calculated the angles in a flash and aimed for the ground immediately in front of the crouching man. He fired. The ricochet shot up into the man's groin between his legs. The thug dropped, his screaming louder than the imam's voice that droned from the mosque's minaret—a beacon to draw out his partner.

Almost instantly, the other assassin appeared and dropped to his knees beside the thrashing man. Then his head came up with shock, realization of the trap written in his fearful eyes. Martin fired again. The second man fell forward, his forehead blown away. With one more round, Martin finished off the man in the green jacket.

A frantic hysteria sounded from the street around the mosque, only sixty meters away from the carnage. Martin pocketed his Browning and hurried toward Hali Road. When he reached it, the first worshippers were pushing and shoving through the street, eager to get away from the gunfire.

Dashing from Swiss Plaza, Martin lurched and his ankle gave way. He caught himself and spied a young man getting on a moped three meters ahead. He called out and the man turned. "I need a ride to my car," Martin said.

"No way." The young man started the little engine and began creeping into the crowd.

"I'll pay you."

The moped screeched to a halt. Martin took out two thousand rupees, and the boy waited while he got on behind and gave him directions. Then the boy gave the vehicle some gas, and the moped chugged down the street, weaving between the devotees and the cars until they reached Radio Pakistan.

The Panther of Baracoa

Martin leapt off the moped and dove into the Mercedes. Then he unzipped the pocket of his backpack to make the duct-taped cola cans accessible. He wired the car, put on his seat belt, and edged to the curb of the car park. He scanned the street. No sign of pursuit.

Relieved, he made a left into the flow of traffic leading away from the area. He'd done it. Farah had the USB on its way to his mother in England, and the thugs had no doubt contacted Lewis when they spotted him at the FedEx. MI6 would find the decoy, and it would take them days to realize nothing was on it.

Martin stopped at the red light at the corner of the street that would take him to Bolan Road and out of town to the train station in Kolpur. He heaved a sigh, and then he glanced across the street. His heart stopped.

Lewis was staring straight at him through the windscreen of his car.

Chapter Thirteen

BLOODY HELL! MARTIN ROUNDED THE CORNER WITH one hand on the wheel and the other opening the sunroof. Horns blared. In the mirror, he saw Lewis cut across traffic against the light to make chase, only three cars behind. Martin snatched a duct-taped cola can from the backpack and pushed the cigarette lighter in the dashboard.

Cars in front of him slowed for a red light. Holding the can and the wheel in the same hand, Martin veered left and cut across the car park of a petrol station at the corner. Lewis followed, still three car lengths behind. With a sharp right, Martin sped toward the intersection. He lit the fuse on the can and threw it out the sunroof to land in the center of the crossing. Smoke jetted from the top of the can.

Tires screeched and the sound of crunching metal filled the air. Martin wove through the traffic and shot free of the confusion. Lewis was no longer behind him, but the man was sure to have called in his thugs. Martin urgently sought a side street. The block was long.

Finally reaching a corner, he veered hard to the left. Governor House rose ahead of him to his right, surrounded

The Panther of Baracoa

by a tall cinder-block fence. He checked his rearview mirror and spotted a Toyota truck zigzagging through the traffic behind him with two men in it. Martin lit another smoke bomb and tossed it through the sunroof.

It exploded and chaos ensued. In his mirror, he saw the truck jolt over the curb and race up the sidewalk around the smoke. Pedestrians screamed and scattered. An old jewelry vendor startled, his wares flying every direction. The truck crushed the man under its wheels, then rocketed back out onto the road.

Martin searched ahead and his grip tightened. Thirty meters in front of him, traffic was deadlocked. He cranked the wheel hard to the right, into the driveway of Governor House. He burst through the gates, jerked the wheel back to the left, and sped across the groomed lawn. Guards ran out from the house, firing their rifles. A bullet smashed the Mercedes' back window. The truck wove into view close behind.

The thug in the passenger seat leaned out the window and fired. Gas streamed from a bullet hole in a propane tank near an outbuilding fifteen meters in front of Martin. He swerved left into another driveway heading for the street. The thug at the window fired again. The propane tank exploded.

A fireball filled the rearview mirror. Martin threw himself down. The vehicle lurched, propelled into oncoming traffic. Brakes squealed. Metal smashed on metal. The air bag deployed, slamming him against the seat. Martin's world spun and crashed to a hard stop against a tree.

He blinked and shook his head, dazed, his ears ringing. He looked back out the shattered window. Fifteen meters away, the truck with the thugs, crushed and flaming, was propped sideways against the stone surround.

Mansion guards streamed toward the chaos, rifles ready. Martin opened his door and grabbed hold of the door frame to keep from spilling out of the car. A man appeared at his side, and Martin reached to the seat beside him for his pistol. It wasn't there.

"Are you hurt?"

Martin studied the stranger. A concerned passerby. "I don't think so. Just a moment." He pushed past the air bag and found his backpack on the floor, the Browning beside it. He discreetly slipped the gun into the pack and zipped it up. Then he allowed the man to help him from the car.

People were emerging from vehicles around him. Some of them were bleeding. Some were crying out.

"Do you need a doctor?" the man asked.

"No. Thank you, but I think those people over there could use some help." Martin pointed toward a woman trying to lift a man from a passenger seat.

The Good Samaritan gave Martin one more look-over and then rushed to help her.

Martin's head spun, and his legs shook like jelly. He turned his back on the flames and wreckage and pushed his way through the crowd that had gathered, limping up the least congested street toward a bus stop.

Enough with being prey. Time to become the predator.

Chapter Fourteen

MARTIN PAID THE DRIVER AND WAITED UNTIL THE TAXI rounded the block before he blended into the pressing darkness of Quetta's industrial area. With every step, his ankle shrieked its protests. He'd stayed on the move until night fell, and he was almost at his limit.

Fighting off his discomfort, he crept up the alley and inside the back gate of a painting company. It took him no time to locate a ladder and sneak back out, shutting the gate behind him.

Three buildings down, he carefully paced off his distance along the tall chain-link fence that surrounded the Aban Khan Construction Company, until he was certain he was in the security camera's blind spot. He didn't want anyone inside the MI6 safe house tipping off Lewis to his presence. Martin leaned the ladder up against the fence and then climbed.

When he reached the top, he vaulted over the rows of barbed wire, simultaneously pushing the ladder backward to fall away from the fence. He landed on his good leg and

BAYARD & HOLMES

rolled to absorb the impact. The ladder smacked against the dirt with a *whap*.

Back on his feet, he bolted into the darkness behind the construction trucks in the yard and waited, listening. Voices broke the silence. Martin peeked out. Two men strolled toward the carport, where Lewis's Toyota sat with three more cars. They said good night and left in two of the vehicles.

Martin slipped into the shadows of the carport and hunkered down, his Browning ready. Lewis would no doubt send confidential reports to whoever was pulling his strings, and he would want to do it once everyone else had left the building. Martin waited.

Before long, one more man exited the building— William, a communications specialist. When William reached the door of his little Nissan, Martin stepped from the shadows, his Browning leveled.

William took a pace back. "Martin? Weren't you reposted? Is this another bloody security drill already?"

Good. Whatever the reason Lewis was after him, William clearly wasn't a part of it.

"If it wasn't, you'd be dead," Martin said. "Hands on the car."

Martin frisked William and removed his pistol and security key card to the building. "Hands behind your back." He tied William's wrists with cord he'd picked up in a shop that afternoon. Then he opened the back of the Nissan. "Now into the boot with you, and wait quietly until someone comes for you."

"Will do, but could you make it quick? The wife has supper on, and I don't want to be late."

"It might not be up to me this time."

William's stomach growled, and his face fell. "Well, do

74

The Panther of Baracoa

try . . . It's good to see you, Martin. Will you be staying?"

"Not if I can help it. Take care of yourself, man. The wind can blow any direction."

"Yes, well . . . Cheers." William crouched into the boot and lay down. Martin closed it.

Now. Time to sort this out once and for all.

Staying in the shadows, Martin stole toward the front door. He entered William's key card, knowing a message would pop up on Lewis's computer saying William was coming back in the building. Once inside, Martin drew his pistol and crept up the stairs to the second floor. Rounding the doorway into Lewis's office, he aimed the Browning at the stocky, black-haired station chief.

Lewis looked up from the file he was reading. Then he glanced toward the Glock 9mm at the corner of his desk.

"Ah, ah, ah." Martin took the pistol from the desk and pocketed it. "Stand up. Hands on the wall."

Lewis glared and did as he was told.

"Feet back farther," Martin said, not satisfied until Lewis was off balance. Then Martin frisked the man and removed a Walther PPK from his ankle holster.

Lewis glanced over his shoulder. "Always were the thorough one, weren't you?"

"Obviously. I'm alive . . . Do you have any idea how many people your locals killed trying to get to me?"

Lewis scowled. "I'd have used your mother for the job, but she was busy sucking off a Tali-bugger."

Martin let the insult glance off and considered his approach. Lewis wasn't going to listen to him. Martin would have to help him get to it on his own. "You tried to kill me, yet I'm not killing you. Why do you think that is?"

Lewis growled. "Because you don't know what I know."

"I don't know what bullshit story you've been given, but

you're now working for the wrong side. Can't you see that? If I were lying, you'd be dead by now. Someone upstairs has betrayed us all. Who is giving you your orders?"

"Of course you would claim that. Did you kill William like you killed our men?"

"Willie's safe in the carport, except for being hungry. As for our men, do you mean that trash you sent after me?"

"You know exactly the men I mean. Keaton, Barclay, Rodgers—all dead because of you."

Hearing their names was a kick in Martin's gut—his men that had been killed in the ambush. He had no idea who the traitor was, but if Lewis believed it was Martin, it was no wonder the ponce was so determined to kill him.

But who pinned that on him, and why? And what could that have to do with the USB drive? Edurne said this involved the EU, the United States, the United Kingdom, Mexico, and even Russia.

Martin frowned. If he couldn't convince Lewis he was mistaken, Martin would have no choice but to disappear— leave behind Farah and everything else he loved, right when he was finally ready to embrace them.

Martin kept his voice calm and low. "Are you blind, man? We've both been betrayed. I know you don't like my intemperate ways, but think. What could anyone possibly offer me? Women? Power? Money? I'd have that and more staying home and going into the family business."

Lewis studied Martin, and Martin could almost see the wheels turning in the other man's head, summing up their history together. Then Lewis's eyes met Martin's and softened.

He gets it!

Martin smiled. "Good man. I knew you could rise above your beginnings."

The Panther of Baracoa

Even as Martin said it, he knew it was a mistake. The wall slammed down, and Lewis's face grew hard. "Bugger off, you ponce. I always knew you'd turn. We intercepted that USB drive with the proof, and we'll have it decrypted within the day. The foreign secretary himself is on to you, so you might as well eat that gun because all of MI6 will hunt you down. Every city, every mountain, every jungle, we'll be there waiting for you. You have slept your last, you filthy wanker."

The foreign secretary? Was that who was behind this? If so, then Lewis was right. No corner of the world would be safe.

Lewis shot him a look of hatred, and Martin's heart sank. The man was in a place where reason couldn't reach him. Perhaps Martin could still plant a seed of doubt.

He gestured toward the wall with the tip of his pistol. "Lean your weight on your head and put your hands behind your back."

With a final glare, Lewis put his head to the wall.

Martin tied his wrists. "You're a good man, Lewis, but you never could see past the end of your elitist peasant nose to know who your true friends are. Now sit down and make yourself comfortable. Hands behind the chair, and don't forget that I own you right now. Ask yourself tomorrow why I didn't kill you, and maybe you'll figure it out before *they* kill you."

Lewis sat. Martin looped the rope around his middle, making sure it was loose enough that the man wouldn't smother. Then he secured Lewis's hands to the back of the chair. He picked up the station chief's car keys and dangled them in front of him. "Feel free to report me to the local authorities once you're free. That is, if you really want them crawling around your safe house."

77

Lewis spat, and Martin twisted out of the way. The spittle hit the wall. Martin slipped away from the desk, shut off the light, and closed the office door behind him. He exited the building to the carport, where he left William's key card under his windscreen wiper. A knocking came from the boot, and William called, "Hello? Is it okay out there?"

Martin stopped himself from reassuring the man and climbed into Lewis's Toyota. He paused and took a deep breath. Where to? Planes and trains were out. Hostiles north, west, and south. East to India was all that was left, perhaps to friends in Nainital, but everything that might have resolved the situation lay back in England—the place he had to avoid at all cost.

At least the USB should be safe with Mother soon. Controlling and difficult as she was, he could trust her.

He glanced at the *Apex Invictus* ring on his finger and remembered how she went half mad when his father died thirty years ago. Though Martin was only four at the time, he could still recall the destruction of her depression and insanity—Kali incarnate. She would suffer deeply at his disappearance, but it couldn't be helped. MI6 would be all over her now. *I'm so sorry, Mother.*

And Farah . . . A deep sadness settled on him, and he sighed.

Come now. It is what it is. They're strong, and so are you.

Martin opened the box under the dashboard and located the fuse to the car's transponder. He popped it out to prevent anyone from tracking him. Then, without a backward glance, he started the engine and sped through the front gate toward Bolan Road and the coming winter.

Chapter Fifteen

Baroness Annaleigh Wentworth Blackburn stared into the fire and drew her gray cashmere cardigan close. She was tired of the cold autumn rain that streamed down outside the arched study windows. It wouldn't matter if she were young; it wouldn't matter if the sun were shining. All that mattered was that Martin hadn't come home. He was often away for long periods of time, but he always came home when he said he would. He knew how she needed that from him.

What happened, dear boy?

She was thrilled when the FedEx envelope had arrived at the Apex Banking Alliance corporate office, but then she had found nothing in it but a USB drive of photographs and an ominous note written in Martin's hand. *Recipe for cooked goose.* It was all she could do not to panic. That had been three long weeks ago.

The flames burned low in the fireplace, and the air grew colder. Annaleigh considered calling a servant but then took up the poker and stirred the fire herself. It calmed her a bit. Nothing like a hot wood fire to cool the soul.

She paced over behind the Louis XVI writing table in front of the window. Rather than sitting, she stared at the mounted grizzly bear head across from her and thought of being with Martin in the Yukon. She had bagged the bear, but the true pleasure was the time she had spent with her son.

She paced the room as restlessness reared up again inside her. Then she stopped. *Come now, pull it together. Martin needs you.*

She sat at her desk and opened her email. Nothing. Still no clue from the head of Apex corporate security about what was on the USB drive buried beneath those photos. But something had to be there, and it had to be the key to Martin's disposition.

A knock sounded at the door, and her tall, elderly butler entered the room. "Director of security at Apex is here to see you, madam. He says it's most urgent."

Annaleigh's heart leapt, but she held her face impassive. "Thank you, Percival. Put another log on the fire and then send him in. See that we're not disturbed."

"Yes, madam." The butler built up the blaze and then exited the room.

A moment later, a large, middle-aged Black man in a suit entered, carrying a manila envelope.

Annaleigh folded her hands together and faced him. "Yes, Wilson?" She always appreciated her interactions with the man. Not only was he capable and efficient, he had been Martin's commanding officer in the Balkans before he retired from the Royal Navy and came to work for her.

Wilson waited to speak until he stood directly in front of the desk. His tones were hushed. "I've completed the decryption. My report, Martin's note, and the drive are in here." He handed her the envelope. It was sealed.

The Panther of Baracoa

Annaleigh slid her letter opener under the flap. "Give me the short version now, please."

Wilson hesitated. "With all due respect, it's best if I don't."

Annaleigh raised an eyebrow, waiting for his explanation.

The large man glanced out the window and then back to her. "You'll understand when you read my report. This is the only copy. I suggest you read it and then immediately destroy it."

Was that fear in his eyes? "Thank you, Wilson. I will take that under advisement."

"I must also ask that, regardless of what you do with this information, we never speak of this matter again. You will find my resignation in the envelope, effective immediately. I am sorry, Baroness. It's been a pleasure to serve you, but I have to think of my family."

She set down the letter opener and pierced her gaze through the man. "This is rather sudden. I assume you have someone in mind for your replacement?"

Wilson shifted and cleared his throat. "Apologies, Baroness, but that won't be possible."

Annaleigh's face tightened and she narrowed her eyes. Some cheek Wilson had. "So you're simply going to abandon your duties? This won't reflect well in my recommendation."

"I understand, madam. I think you will understand, as well, when you read my report."

She pursed her lips. "That will be all."

She watched his back retreat through the door. What could possibly inspire such a radical move on the part of the seasoned veteran? She steadied herself and then emptied the contents of the envelope onto her desk—the USB drive, the four words from Martin, a single page of handwritten block print, and Wilson's resignation.

She read the report, and her stomach churned. Then, she read it again. *How can this be? So many enemies in one bed!*

She set down the paper, and the morbid truth overwhelmed her. Annaleigh's blood ran cold. Her son had to be dead. If he knew anything about this, they could never let him live.

My boy! They must have hunted you down like a rabid dog.

She stared at the picture of him at the corner of her desk. Tears blurred her vision, and the image of his jaunty smile and ruffled blond hair offered only pain. An abyss of grief gaped open in her heart, and despair threatened to consume her.

She thought of Martin's courage and how he had always put his mission first. That was what he would expect from her. That was why he had sent her the drive instead of someone else. He counted on her to do something, and she would not disappoint him.

She straightened in her chair. Blinking back her tears, she read the report one last time, memorizing every word. Then she crumpled the paper and clenched it in her fists.

She crossed to the mantel, knelt in front of the fire, and pulled up the sleeve of her cardigan. Then she carefully positioned the paper deep inside the blaze, ignoring the heat on her hand. She leaned back and stared at the yellow tongues flicking up. They caught the ball and, with a bright burst, devoured it whole.

Like the world going up in flames.

Mesmerized by the dancing flares of light, her grief gave way to anger, igniting and building inside her. Her mind

The Panther of Baracoa

raced, dark thoughts searing and smoldering until finally shifting and forming an idea—a bitter purpose. She spoke into the flames. "I will avenge you, Martin. I can't stop them, but as God is my witness, I will burn down their world."

Annaleigh stood and smoothed her skirt, determination alight in her spirit. She crossed to her desk and pressed a button on it. Percival appeared in the doorway. Annaleigh set her chin. "Call a game together for the weekend. We're going to raise the stakes."

Truth and Fiction

1. Is there a black market for Cuban cocoa?

There was until a few years ago. American mobsters smuggled Cuban cocoa out of Baracoa, a centuries-old smugglers' haven, and across the Dominican Republic to Puerto Rico. Once there, they had illegal workers in factories concealed in dairy farms make chocolate using Puerto Rican sugar. They counterfeited labels of top chocolate companies and sold the chocolate in the United States and Europe. Eventually, Havana recognized that it was better off allowing the cocoa farmers to accept foreign currency for the cocoa, and then the dictator's flunkies would at least get a cut by way of taxes and bribes.

2. Can you really make smoke bombs with waxed paper, cola cans, sugar, gunpowder, and matches?

Yes. But don't do this at home. If you do it just right, it will work, but if you don't, you're likely to set fire to yourself and/or your mom's home. (We assume you're living with your mom if you have the time on your hands to make homemade smoke bombs.)

3. Is an intelligence organization killing one of its own as common as films make it out to be?

Absolutely not. It's very serious business to go after one of your own, and it would only happen under the direst circumstances, such as when numerous agents or civilians are at risk and there is no other way to stop the person. See *Spycraft: Essentials* for more on this topic.

4. Would an operative have a personal life that he kept completely hidden from his peers?

Yes. As Frederick Forsyth said about Foreign Secretary Robin Cook, "If a man cannot keep a measly affair secret, what is he doing in charge of the Intelligence Service?" See *Spycraft: Essentials* for more on this topic.

5. It seems everyone in this story has a price. Is that realistic?

Not everyone does, but members of the business community are used to trading cash for services, and haggling is more common outside of the English-speaking world. Also, people in these areas see more outsiders and are generally more open to making deals with strangers.

The Panther of Baracoa

———

If you have other questions for us, please send us an email at bayardandholmes@protonmail.com, and we would be happy to answer if we legally and ethically are able to do so.

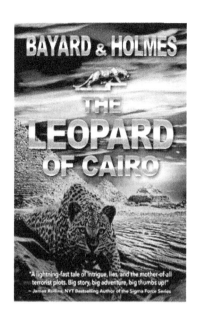

THE LEOPARD OF CAIRO

John Viera leaves his CIA fieldwork hoping for a "normal" occupation and a long-awaited family. But when a Pakistani engineer is kidnapped from a top-secret US project and diplomatic entanglements tie the government's hands, the Intelligence Community turns to John and his team of ex-operatives to investigate—*strictly off the books*. They uncover a plot of unprecedented magnitude that will precipitate the slaughter of millions.

From the corporate skyscrapers of Montreal to the treacherous alleys of Baluchistan, these formidable enemies strike, determined to create a regional apocalypse and

The Panther of Baracoa

permanently alter the balance of world power. Isolated in their knowledge of the impending devastation, John and his network stand alone between total destruction and *The Leopard of Cairo*.

"Here is a lightning-fast tale of intrigue, lies, and the mother-of-all terrorist plots. Big story, big adventure, big thumbs-up!"
—James Rollins, *New York Times* Bestselling Author of the Sigma Force series

"Delicious tradecraft, elegantly plotted. The Leopard of Cairo is Bayard and Holmes best one yet. An excellent reminder that great spies tell great stories. Do not miss the Truth and Fiction section at the back."
—Annie Jacobsen, Bestselling Author of *Surprise, Kill, Vanish* and

TV writer/producer of Tom Clancy's *Jack Ryan*

Acknowledgments

Our abiding gratitude to Julee Schwarzburg, who is the editor of our dreams and the difference between writing an actual thriller and playing with imaginary friends.

Our humble indebtedness to Vicki Hinze, friend and mentor extraordinaire. She is our earth angel.

Our deepest thanks to John Cladianos, Susan Spann, Doug Patteson, David Sylvian, Jen Bullington, Kristen Lamb, Kerry Meacham, K.B. Owen, Nigel Blackwell, and Donna Collins for their unflagging support through this endeavor. Their constant friendship and advice has been indispensable through the years, and they are true blessings.

Our sincerest love and appreciation to our families, who tolerated our loud laughter at 3 a.m. and cheered us on through every unforeseen obstacle, of which there were many. They are the home we dream of as we sail our journeys.

Our undying gratitude to you, our readers. You make our efforts worthwhile.

Thank you, one and all.

About the Authors

Piper Bayard is an author and a recovering attorney. She is also a belly dancer, a mom, and a former hospice volunteer. She currently pens espionage fiction and nonfiction with Jay Holmes, as well as her own science fiction.

Jay Holmes is a forty-something-year veteran of field intelligence operations spanning from the Cold War fight against the Soviets, the East Germans, and the terrorist organizations they sponsored to the present Global War on Terror. Piper is the public face of their partnership.

Together, Bayard & Holmes author nonfiction articles and books on espionage and foreign affairs, as well as fictional spy thrillers. They are the bestselling authors of *Spycraft: Essentials*.

When they aren't writing or, in Jay's case, busy with "other work," Piper and Jay are enjoying their families, hiking, exploring, talking foreign affairs, laughing at their own rude jokes, and questing for the perfect chocolate cake recipe. If you think you have that recipe, please share it with them at their email below.

To receive notices of upcoming Bayard & Holmes releases, subscribe to the Bayard & Holmes Covert Briefing. Contact Bayard & Holmes at their website Bayardand-Holmes.com, at their email, BayardandHolmes@protonmail.com, or at @piperbayard on Twitter.

Made in United States
North Haven, CT
19 January 2024

47674102R00059